DENNIS the MENACE

THE COMPLETE MENACE!

BEANObooks

published under licence by

meadowside
CHILDREN'S BOOKS

CONTENTS

SPORTS DAY

Dennis had tried his best to get out of it.

"I'm hearing voices," he said at breakfast. "I'm infectious. I've lost my toes. My brain fell out. Gnasher ate my sports kit."

"Only because you fed it to him," said Mum.

"And you're not getting out of sports day," Dad added.

Dennis groaned. Usually he loved sports day. He looked forward to the competitions. He looked forward to being the fastest and the strongest. Most of all he looked forward to getting as muddy as he possibly could.

But this sports day was going to be different. Mr Pump, the new sports teacher, had said that everyone who got muddy would have to have a hot, soapy shower afterwards. Dennis had argued and raged. He had tried every excuse he could think of. But Mr Pump would not change his mind.

There was only one thing for it. Dennis was going to have to avoid mud. And that didn't sound like any fun at all.

"I've never had to shower before," Dennis grumbled.

This was true. His old sports teacher had always been very glad not to have Dennis anywhere near the shower room.

"Well, your new teacher must be very keen," said Mum. "Anyway, it's about time you had a wash. I've given up trying to get you into a bath."

Dennis scowled.

"Now," Mum continued, "I want you to try your best today, Dennis. We'll be watching you, cheering you on..."

"...and making sure you don't get up to any menacing," Dad finished.

Later that morning Dennis stood outside the boys' changing room, glowering. There must be some menacing way he could put a stop to sports day. He reached into his pocket and his hand closed around a small tin.

"Perfect," grinned Dennis. It was his spare tin of itching powder. He crept into the teachers' changing room and saw Mr Pump's shorts hanging on a peg. Dennis emptied his tin into the shorts and smiled.

Once his teacher put those on, he would not be able to stand still, and without him sports day would be cancelled. Dennis went back to his changing room and waited for the good news.

But when Mr Pump strode into the boys' changing room, he was wearing a tracksuit! Dennis frowned. His first menace was ruined. What next?

Mr Pump watched as everyone shuffled out to the sports field. He was tall and tanned, with a huge chest and enormous muscles. His legs were like tree trunks and his head was large and square. Even the other teachers kept away from him.

"He's much too keen for this school," snarled Mr Dobson.

"He told me he loves teaching," complained Mr Plink. "The man must be mad."

"I heard him say he likes the children," added Miss Toffy. "Completely unnatural."

"He'll never last," barked the headmistress.

All the parents were arriving and waving to their children. Dennis saw Mum and Dad and scowled at them.

"R-I-G-H-T,"

shouted Mr Pump through his microphone. Everyone winced and covered their ears. "The first event will be the egg-and-spoon race!"

The ten kids who were taking part stood on the starting line with their spoons. Some of them looked eager. Some of them looked miserable. Dennis looked furious.

Mr Pump walked along the row, putting an egg into every spoon from his basket. Dennis was the last to get an egg. Mr Pump put the egg basket down next to him.

"Mistake number one," grinned Dennis. If he couldn't get sports day cancelled, perhaps he could get himself banned from it! He reached down to the egg basket. Mr Pump held the starting pistol up in the air.

"On your marks!"

Dennis grabbed handfuls of eggs.

"Get set!"

Dennis got his throwing arm in position.

"GO!"

Nine kids surged forward, balancing their eggs. One menace stayed still and fired.

POW!

Plug fell down and cut his knee on some eggshell.

SPLAT!

Smiffy tripped and smashed his egg.

BONK!

Cuthbert was knocked dizzy by a hard-boiled egg.

Dennis kept firing until the only egg left was the one in his spoon. He stepped over the yolk-splattered children and crossed the finish line. The crowd hissed.

"That was not how you run an
egg-and-spoon race!" shouted Mr
Pump. "These children will have to
go home – they aren't fit to join in
any more events!"

"Am I going to be banned?" asked Dennis hopefully.

"Oh no," smiled Mr Pump. "I'm not that cruel!"

Dennis sighed. Menace number two hadn't worked. What now?

"It's the pole vault next!" Mr Pump announced. "Line up, everyone taking part! Dennis, hold the mat steady please."

There was a big mud puddle right next to the thick blue mat. As soon as the first competitor vaulted over the bar, Dennis would get splattered! He pulled the mat across to cover the puddle, just as Bertie Blenkinsop started his vault.

16

Bertie landed on the hard ground. "Owwww! My botty!" Bertie squealed. **"Silly boy,"** snapped Mr Pump. "How did you miss the mat? Next!"

Spotty was next, but just then Dennis saw another muddy puddle. He tugged the mat again. **C-R-U-N-C-H-!** Spotty landed on his nose.

There were dozens of muddy puddles! Dennis pulled and tugged at the mat to try to cover them all. **C-R-A-C-K!** Curly landed on Spotty.

17

E-E-K-! Pie Face fell face down in the mud.

"Very poor show!" frowned Mr Pump as Pie Face limped off to the shower room. "Your turn, Dennis."

Dennis glowered at the sports teacher and started to run up to the bar. But as he ran he saw another huge puddle – right in front of him! He shoved the pole into the ground and vaulted high over the bar, landing WHUMP in the middle of the mat.

"Very good!" said Mr Pump. "The winner of the pole vault is... Dennis!"

"Well done!" called a proud Mum and Dad.

"Boo!" shouted everyone else.

"Next it's the cross-country race," boomed Mr Pump.

"Oh no," groaned Dennis. There

was nothing he liked better than splashing through deep muddy fields. But he wouldn't go into those showers!

"This could take a while," continued Mr Pump, "so there are some refreshments for the parents in the gym."

This was what the parents had been waiting for. There was a stampede for the gym. No one saw the race start. And no one saw Dennis sneak off in completely the wrong direction.

Dennis spotted Mr Pump's mountain bike in the staff car park. He rubbed his hands together. "I think I'm getting one of my brilliant ideas."

The kids running over the muddy fields just saw a blur as Dennis whizzed past them on the mountain bike. He stopped at the first crossroads and chuckled. There was a big sign that said 'Cross-country Runners this way' and an arrow pointing left.

"How about a little detour?" Dennis grinned. Just because he couldn't get muddy, it was cruel to stop the others getting good and dirty! He turned the arrow so it was pointing right, towards the Beanotown Bog. Then he took the left turn and sped off on the bike.

There was another sign at the next crossroads. Dennis pointed the arrow towards the woods. "It's so easy to get lost round here!" he sniggered. If there were no kids left to compete, they would have to end sports day! And he was still mud free!

When he got back to school, Dennis put the bike back in the staff car park and then jogged over the finish line. All the parents were just coming back from the gym, clutching lemonade and cake.

"Oh I say!" shouted Mr Pump. "Dennis has won the race! And amazingly, he has no mud on him!"

"I can hardly believe it," gasped Mum.

"Neither can I," said Dad grimly. "Not at all."

Mr Pump looked for the rest of the runners. But no one else came over the finish line. (This was not surprising. Seven of them were wading through a bog and two more were lost in the wood.)

"They can't have gone the wrong way," said Mr Pump. "Very strange – I put some very big signs up.

Anyway, let's get on with the next event – the long jump!"

There were only two children doing the long jump – Dennis and Walter. Dennis groaned when he saw the sandpit. It was full of rainwater and the sand was a muddy mess.

"Now, you know the rules,"

shouted Mr Pump. "Take a running jump into the sand. Whoever jumps farthest is the winner. **Good luck!**

You're first, Dennis!"

"There's only one thing for it," Dennis grinned. He hurtled down the runway and whizzed into the air over the sandpit. He jumped so far that he landed on the grass on the other side!

"Astonishing!" said Mr Pump. "I've never seen anything like it! Next please!"

Walter was next. He did some warm-up exercises as Dennis smirked and emptied his pockets into the sand.

"Good luck, Walter!" he called. Walter ignored him. He tottered down the runway, tripped over a daisy, looked down and...

"A-r-r-g-g-h-h!" screamed Walter, trying to keep running in mid air. "Creepy crawlies!"

The muddy sandpit was alive with spiders, worms and beetles. Walter scrabbled out of the sand and kept running.

"COME BACK!" shouted Mr Pump. "Come back or you'll be disqualified!"

But Walter ran into the audience and hid under his mumsy's chair.

"Tch, tch," Mr Pump shook his head. "Odd boy."

There were only two kids left in the whole sports day competition – Dennis and Roger the Dodger.

"Only one to go and it's all over – without needing a shower!" chuckled Dennis.

"Next event!" announced Mr Pump. "It's the shot put! Dennis, would you go first, please?"

"Oh dear," said Mum.

"At least it's not the javelin," muttered Dad.

Dennis grabbed the shot and started to spin, round and round he went, faster and faster, until he launched the shot. It flew through the air...

...towards the parents...

"Good throw!" cried Mr Pump.

...and squashed Walter's mumsy's picnic lunch.

"Bad throw!" shouted Mr Pump.

"GOAL!"

cheered Dennis, punching the air.

He held the second shot out to
Roger, but dropped it. The shot
landed on Roger's left foot.

E-E-E-K-!

shrieked Roger, hopping around the field and clutching his foot, which was swelling up like a balloon.

"Oops, butterfingers,"

said Dennis.

Mr Pump frowned. He was starting to think that this hadn't been a success. Slowly he picked up his microphone.

"There are supposed to be five more events," he said. "But there are no more children to compete. Since Dennis is the only one left – I suppose he is the winner!"

Just then Dad came marching up to Mr Pump. He said a few words. Mr Pump nodded vigorously. They both glanced at Dennis. Then they shook hands.

"Step up, Dennis!" bellowed Mr
Pump into his microphone. "You are
the winner of this year's
school sports day."

Mr Pump took out
a big gold medal on a
long blue ribbon. He put
it around Dennis's neck.

Mum clapped. No one else did.

"Thanks," grinned Dennis. He
turned to leave, but something
stopped him. Mr Pump had
tightened the ribbon around his
neck. Dennis couldn't move.

"Not so fast!" he thundered.
"Ladies and gentlemen, we have a
special treat for Dennis. He's such a
sporty lad, I'm sure he'd love to do
some more exercise. So we're going
to let him exercise his hands and
knees. Dennis, you can spend the
rest of the day cleaning out the

shower room – with a toothbrush! And when it's clean, then you can test it out by having a nice, hot, soapy shower!"

There was a huge cheer from the crowd. The parents clapped. The children limping back from the cross-country race whistled and waved. Mr Pump got a standing ovation as he marched Dennis off to the shower room.

The other teachers looked at each other.

"Perhaps we were a bit hasty about Mr Pump," said Mr Dobson.

"He seems like a very nice man," Miss Toffy nodded.

"A splendid addition to the school," agreed Mr Plink.

The headmistress watched Mr Pump hand Dennis a toothbrush.

Then she did something very unusual. She smiled.

"I think he's going to fit right in," she said.

DENNIS THE DIRECTOR

"I'm really bored," said Dennis at breakfast.

Mum and Dad exchanged worried looks. When Dennis said he was bored, it usually meant trouble. Dad fished into his pocket and pulled out a five-pound note.

"Here you are, Dennis. Why don't you treat yourself to a film at the cinema," he said.

Dennis pushed the money into his pocket and gave a wide grin.

"Thanks, Dad!" He crammed the last piece of toast into his mouth and raced out of the door.

"He can't get up to any menacing

while he's watching a film," Dad told Mum.

At his front gate, Dennis bumped into his friends, Curly and Pie Face.

"Come on," he grinned, waving the five-pound note at them. "We're going to the cinema! What film do you wanna see?"

"A scary one!" said Curly and Pie Face at the same time.

They raced to Silver's Super Cinema and joined the queue for tickets. The cinema manager was serving at the ticket counter. His bushy black eyebrows were glowering and there was a scowl on his face. It got even worse when he saw Dennis, Curly and Pie Face.

"Not you lot again," he grumbled. "First my assistant goes off sick so I

have to do some work and now you menaces turn up.

Well, I'm warning you, any trouble and you're out!"

He jerked a thumb over his shoulder. Dennis, Curly and Pie Face just grinned at him and walked into the dark cinema. They went upstairs and sat in the little balcony area, right at the front.

"These are the best seats in the house but everyone always forgets about them," Dennis chuckled. "We'll have the balcony to ourselves!"

They settled down to watch the film. But soon the three menaces began to scowl. The film wasn't scary at all!

"What a rotten trick," whispered Curly. "All these people came here for a good scare, and this film wouldn't even scare a softy!"

"Maybe we should give them their money's worth!" suggested Dennis. "Quick – what have you got in your pockets?"

Curly and Pie Face emptied their pockets at top speed. Between them they had five earwigs, eight spiders, four catapults (Dennis always carried a spare for emergencies), two bird whistles, three feathers and a ball of string. A smile spread over Dennis's face. It was a smile Curly and Pie Face knew very well. It meant that a menace was on the way!

Dennis picked up the feathers and tied a long piece of string to the end of each one. Then they dangled the feathers over the edge of the balcony.

"Arghh!"
"Eeek!"

The people in the row below screamed as they felt the feathers brush the backs of their necks.

Dennis, Curly and Pie Face whipped the feathers out of sight.

"Shhh!" hissed the cinema manager, who couldn't see the feathers in the dark. He thought they were screaming at the film and he didn't like to hear anyone having too much fun.

Next Dennis picked up a bird whistle. He cupped it in his hands and began to make a faint, ghostly, hooting sound. The people in the audience started to turn around, trying to work out where the spooky noise was coming from. Pie Face and Curly stuffed their fists into their mouths to stop giggling. People were holding on to each other and shivering in fear.

"It's ghosts!" quivered one lady.

"A haunted cinema!" trembled her friend.

"This cinema is not haunted!" seethed the manager. But no one was listening to him.

Next Dennis, Pie Face and Curly picked up their catapults together with the earwigs and spiders they had been keeping. TWANG! Dennis sent a spider somersaulting through the air. ZING! An earwig shot from Curly's catapult.

"Arghh!" screamed a man as an earwig landed in his popcorn.

"Help!" squeaked a woman as two spiders dangled from her earrings.

Within seconds everyone was on their feet, jumping around and screaming. On screen the actress had just walked into a haunted house, but the film was completely forgotten. The audience rushed out, fighting to be first through the door. The manager narrowed his eyes. His bushy eyebrows waggled angrily and he looked up at the balcony.

"Oh, ghosts and insects is it?" he muttered furiously. "That really is the last straw!"

He ran up to the balcony three steps at a time and grabbed Curly and Pie Face by the collars, yelling as he dragged them downstairs.

"You menaces are banned once and for all!" he bellowed as he dragged them through the angry crowd of people, who were all demanding their money back.

"You shouldn't show such boring films, then!" Dennis roared as he followed Pie Face and Curly out to the street. They had been dropped in a muddy puddle. The manager slammed the door behind them and

Dennis stomped off down the street.

"We've gotta teach that old bully a lesson!" he stormed. Then he skidded to a halt. A crowd of softies was gathered on the pavement ahead. Walter was there with Spotty Perkins and Bertie Blenkinsop.

"What's going on here?" Dennis asked. Walter turned around.

"Oh it's you riff-raff!" he said rudely. "This is not for menaces like you, Dennis."

"Oh yeah?" growled Dennis. Softies went flying right and left as he elbowed his the way through the crowd. He saw a large poster on the wall.

HOLLYWOOD COMES TO BEANOTOWN

A CHANCE TO BE A DIRECTOR

MAKE YOUR OWN FILM AND WIN A FANTASTIC PRIZE!

"Excellent!" grinned Dennis. "If we can't watch films any more, we can make 'em!"

"Haw haw," sneered Walter. "As if a menace like you knows anything about directing! I'm going to make a film about scented flowers and twittering birds and pretty trees. If I'm very lucky, I might even see a fairy at the bottom of my garden!"

"There's no such thing as fairies!" scoffed Dennis.

"What?" squeaked one of the softies in dismay.

"Don't listen to him," said Walter. "My film is going to be the best, and with Mumsy's super-duper new video camera I am bound to win!"

"With a film about flowers and fairies!" guffawed Dennis. "Fat chance!"

He turned to Pie Face and Curly. "There's no way a softy's gonna beat us!" he said, thumping his fist into his palm.

"Come on, menaces – were gonna be film directors!"

They raced back to Dennis's house and found Dad's old video camera in a box under the stairs. It was held together with elastic bands and sticky tape.

"It's falling to bits!" Curly complained.

"It's what you film that counts – not the camera!" grinned Dennis. "And Walter's flowers can't beat what we're about to film!"

"What's that?" asked Pie Face.

"Menacing!" Dennis said.

45

Dennis, Curly and Pie Face had a busy week.

On Monday they filmed his neighbour the Colonel. Dennis and Curly crept into his garden, where he was putting his soldier dolls through their paces.

"Hup two three four! Hup two three four! Keep marching!" the Colonel bellowed. Dennis grinned into the camera lens.

"This is the Colonel," he whispered into the microphone. "He's as nutty as a fruitcake!"

"I heard that!" roared the Colonel, grabbing Dennis by the scruff of the neck and giving him a shake.

"You little menace!"

"Gnasher, quick!" shouted Dennis. Gnasher leapt up and took a huge bite out of the seat of the Colonel's trousers. He shot into the air, clutching his bottom and letting go of Dennis.

"**RUN!**" Dennis yelled. "Keep filming, Curly!"

The Colonel chased Dennis through all the back gardens, leaping over fences as if they were hurdles in a race.

"Come back here! You'll be court-martialled!" the Colonel thundered. Dennis shot through a small gap in a fence, closely followed by Gnasher, Curly and Pie Face. The Colonel was so angry he didn't stop! He threw himself  into the gap and got stuck halfway through. On one side of the fence his legs kicked in the air, while on the other his nose was tickled by Dennis's mum's sunflowers!

"You stop that filming at once – **ACHOO!** – and get me out of here!" the Colonel stormed. But Dennis and his cameramen were disappearing into the distance!

On Tuesday they filmed Walter the Softy. He was out for a walk with his girlfriend Matilda and they passed Dennis's house. Dennis was just spraying Curly with the garden hose when he heard Walter's voice.

"These are for you, Matilda," he said. "I picked them myself!"

Dennis and Curly peered over the garden hedge. Walter had just handed Matilda a bunch of flowers, tied with a pink ribbon.

"Yuck!" said Curly, sticking out his tongue.

"You're so wonderful, Walter," said Matilda. "I'll put them in some water to keep them fresh and beautiful, just like me."

"Ugghh!" cried Dennis, "I've heard enough!" He switched on the hose and blasted the bunch of flowers with it. "That'll keep 'em wet – and you too!" he chortled. Walter and Matilda were soaked from head to foot!

"You scoundrel!" spluttered Matilda. "You've ruined my hairstyle and it took Mumsy hours this morning!"

"Well, all little flowers need watering!" guffawed Curly.

On Wednesday they filmed Sergeant Slipper. Roger the Dodger lent them one of his best dodges – a pound coin on the end of a fishing line. They put it on the pavement where Sergeant Slipper walked on his beat. When he saw the pound he bent down eagerly to grab it, but Dennis jerked the fishing rod and the pound leapt away from the policeman.

"Oy, come back here!" he bellowed, chasing the pound coin. But every time he bent to pick it up, it was whisked out of his reach.

Sergeant Slipper chased the pound

coin all the way through Beanotown. He splashed through muddy puddles and charged through crowds, sending people flying in all directions.

"Must... get... the money..." he puffed. His blue uniform was splattered with mud and his helmet was wonky, but he didn't care. All he wanted was to catch that pound!

With one final determined roar he leapt through the air at the coin... and sprawled at the feet of the Chief Inspector!

"**SLIPPER!**" roared the Chief Inspector. "What is the meaning of this?"

Dennis pulled the coin out of sight and raced off with Curly and Pie Face, chortling.

On Thursday they filmed Minnie the Minx. There was a party in her garden because her cousin was getting married and Minnie was wearing a pink frilly dress!

"Look at Minnie!" hooted Dennis, filming her over the fence.

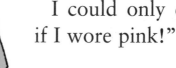

"I think she's turned into a softy!" tittered Pie Face.

"Grrr!" snarled Minnie. "I had to wear a dress to get all the lovely grub – Mum said I could only eat it if I wore pink!"

54

"A likely story!" chuckled Dennis. Minnie clenched her fists.

"I'll show you I'm not a softy!" she growled. She leapt over the fence to chase them – straight into next door's pile of manure!

"Pwoaar, what a pong!" cried Dennis, holding his nose.

"Frilly and stinky!" grinned Pie Face.

Just then Minnie's mum peered over the fence. When she saw Minnie she went purple in the face.

55

"I warned you!" she spluttered.
"Up to your room, right now!
There'll be no party food for you!"

On Friday they filmed Bea. She
wanted to repaint her room and
Dennis agreed to help her. They lined
up pots of yellow, red and green
paint.

"Ready, Bea?" asked Dennis.

"GO!" squealed Bea.

Dennis picked her up and dipped her hands and feet into the green paint. Then he held her up to the wall so that she could make her own patterns!

"More!" Bea shouted. They did the same with the red and yellow paint, until all the walls were covered with a bright new design. Bea clapped her paint-covered hands together. She crawled out of her room and downstairs. Dennis grabbed the camera and followed her.

"That's right, Bea!" he chortled, as she crawled around the sitting room. "Mum's always saying she wants the house redecorated!"

Soon every room in the house was covered with green, yellow and blue handprints and footprints.

"Nice!" cooed Bea.

"EEEK!" screamed Mum as she walked in and dropped all her shopping bags. "DENNIS!"

But Dennis and Bea had vanished!

At last it was time to watch the finished films. The whole of Beanotown crammed into the cinema. The judge was Mr Silver, the owner of the cinema.

While all the softies' films were playing, Mr Silver's eyes kept drooping. During Walter's film, he started to snore after the fortieth shot of a geranium. At last there was only one film left to watch. The title flashed up on the screen:

A MENACE STRIKES BACK!

The audience gasped as the film opened with a shot of the Colonel stuck halfway through the garden fence with his nose in a sunflower.

"There's only one good use for flowers when you're a menace," said Dennis's voiceover. Mr Silver roared with laughter. The Colonel said "Hurrumph!" very loudly from the back of the cinema.

They watched as the film unfolded. When Minnie landed in the manure, Mr Silver had to wipe tears of laughter from his eyes. As the film ended and the lights came up, he leaned over and shook Dennis by the hand.

"A hilarious film, young man! Takes me back to my youth!"

"And what about my little darling's film?" trumpeted Walter's mumsy crossly.

Mr Silver cleared his throat and stood up to address the audience.

"There have been some, er, interesting entries," he said. "I think we have all learned a lot of things about geraniums that we never knew before."

"And never wanted to know!" added Dennis in a loud whisper. Mum threw him a warning look.

"But there is a clear winner," Mr Silver continued. "A hilarious comedy film, where the acting was so real I could almost believe that people were actually being menaced! Congratulations lads – the prize goes to Dennis, Curly and Pie Face!"

There was loud applause from their parents and angry mutterings from everyone else. The Colonel tried to say something but only let out a strange, gurgling sound.

"The prize is a wonderful one for budding film makers," continued Mr Silver. "Free tickets for a year into my cinema!"

"Awesome!" cheered Dennis.

"Mega!" shouted Pie Face and Curly.

"Oh no," groaned the manager, burying his head in his hands.

Dennis, Curly and Pie Face went up to Mr Silver to collect their prizes. He shook their hands and congratulated them again. "But there's one thing I want to know," he said. "How did you get all those people to pretend to be menaced in your film?"

"Oh, that was easy," chortled Dennis. "It just came naturally!"

GNASHER'S CARNIVAL CHAOS

"Oh, Gno," muttered Gnasher to himself. He was worried. He and Dennis were supposed to be going to the carnival with Curly and Pie Face, but Mum was holding onto his collar very tightly, and Gnasher had a horrible feeling that he knew why.

"Gnasher's staying here with me," she said.

"No way!"

bellowed Dennis.

"This Tripe Hound needs a bath – it is two years since his last one and he's starting to attract flies," said Mum firmly.

"But I like this smell!" Gnasher thought. It had taken him two years to build up the perfect odour and now Mum wanted to take it away from him!

Dennis raged and Gnasher struggled, but in the end Dennis had to go without him. Mum let go of Gnasher to pull on her thickest pair of rubber gloves. Then she turned to him and put her hands on her hips.

"Right," she said through gritted teeth. "I'm not looking forward to this any more than you are. But by the time I'm finished with you, you're going to smell like roses."

"Oh, yeah?" growled Gnasher. "Wanna bet?"

The great chase began! Gnasher weaved through chair legs and crawled under sofas. He balanced on the curtain rail and tried to climb up the chimney. He kicked cushions under Mum's feet and attempted to escape through the letterbox. But it was no use. Finally Mum clutched him in a grip of iron, marched into the bathroom and locked the door.

It was a very unpleasant half hour indeed.

At the end of it, Mum unlocked the bathroom door. She was covered in soot, soap, black hairs and water. Gnasher raced downstairs. He was dripping with water and smelled equally of roses and wet dog. Dad saw him coming and opened the front door to let him out. Gnasher pounded down the garden path with a wild look in his eyes.

"Phew!" said Dad as Mum crawled out of the bathroom on her hands and knees. "What's that horrible pong?"

"Tea and lots of it!" gibbered Mum. "I'm not doing that for another two years at least!"

Gnasher pelted down the street, filled with shame. The scent of roses followed him wherever he went! He splashed through muddy puddles and rolled in all the dirt he could find. But somehow the strong smell of roses would not leave. By the time he reached the centre of Beanotown, he was fuming. And that was when he spotted Foo-Foo.

Usually, Foo-Foo would have smelt Gnasher coming, but this time he didn't notice a thing. Gnasher crept up behind him on the tips of his toes. He waited until he was right behind him before letting out a loud

"GNASH!"

Perhaps this rosy smell had some benefits after all! Foo-Foo shot into the air like a rocket and landed in Walter's arms, quivering.

"Bad dog!" cried Walter. Gnasher bared his teeth and grabbed a mouthful of Walter's pink socks.

"Eeek!"

Walter squealed, trying to run away.

"Let me go, you horrid beast! I have to get to the dog show at the carnival!"

"Dog show! Gnash!" barked Gnasher. "That's for softy dogs!"

He chased after Walter and Foo-Foo. They ran to the field where the carnival was being held. Gnasher lost sight of them in the crowd, but he didn't care. There were more ankles to bite here than he had ever seen in one place!

Gnasher raced into the crowd with delight, getting ready to practise his best gnawing techniques. He spotted a pair of socks that really deserved gnashing – they were covered with pictures of flowers and kittens, and they belonged to Walter's girlfriend Matilda.

70

But just as Gnasher opened his mouth ready to chomp, he saw  something that stopped him in his tracks. He stayed as if he had been frozen, with one paw in the air and his mouth hanging open. The smell of roses stopped bothering him. He forgot all about the flowery socks. There, straight ahead of him, was a beautiful white Tripe Hound!

Gnasher was smitten! He bounded up to her.

"My name's Gnasher," he began, but she didn't let him finish. She bared her sharp white teeth and growled at him.

71

"I've got no time to talk to Tripe Hounds who smell of roses," she snapped. "I'm a carnival dog, and I've got a dog show to judge!"

"I don't usually smell like this," blushed Gnasher.

"I should hope not! Now clear off and stop bothering me!"

With a powerful back kick, the amazing creature sent Gnasher tumbling back into the crowd. Gnasher sat up and rubbed his head as he watched her leave.

"What a gorgeous kick!" he thought dreamily.

Not far away, Dennis, Pie Face and Curly were busy trying out some carnival games.

First they visited the coconut shy.

"I'll have the first shot," said

Dennis, getting his throwing arm ready. He hit the coconuts so hard that they split open and showered the man in charge with coconut milk. The three menaces guffawed loudly.

The first time it happened the man gave a tight smile and handed over Dennis's prize – a coconut.

The second time (Curly's turn) he didn't smile at all.

And when Pie Face did the same thing he scowled as he wiped coconut milk out of his eyes. Dennis stepped up for another turn. He took aim, fired and... **POW!**

"Clear off, you menaces!" the man roared, as his coconuts were smashed to pieces for the fourth time and he was drenched in coconut milk. "I'm running out of coconuts!"

Next they tried the helter skelter, but
Dennis went so fast that he caught
the other two up on the first bend!
Curly and Pie Face flew
off the helter skelter
and landed on top of
the woman who was
running it.

"You're all
banned!"
she shrieked as soon as
Curly had clambered off her.
In the plate smashing game,
Dennis was unhappy with
the squashy balls they were
given to throw.

"These softy balls don't smash anything!" he complained. His hand reached around to his back pocket. He pulled out his favourite catapult. He pulled out the coconut he had won. Pie Face and Curly chortled as Dennis loaded the coconut into his catapult, aimed at the plates and...

SMASH!

The coconut whizzed through the air, broke half the plates and shot a hole through the back of the stand, which gave a little wobble and folded up like a concertina!

"What a mega menace!" chortled Curly.

GRRRR! began the stand's owner.

"Run!" yelled Pie Face.

When they played hit the rat, Dennis hit it so hard that he broke the game in two. And finally the only thing they hadn't visited was the big top. Some clowns were fooling around by the entrance and there was a big sign over the door that read:

"Ha," scoffed Dennis as he saw Walter the Softy go in with Foo-Foo. "What a load of softy dogs! Who'd want a stupid rosette anyway?"

The others agreed and they started to leave, but Dennis found he couldn't move. When he looked down, he saw that Gnasher had his jumper in a tight grip and was pulling him towards the big top.

"You don't wanna go in there!" cried Dennis in alarm. "It's full of softies! And what's that smell of roses? What has Mum done to you, Gnasher?"

But Gnasher kept pulling.

"Good luck!" chortled Pie Face as Dennis disappeared inside the big top.

"Yeah, enjoy the show, mate!" guffawed Curly as they scarpered. Dennis wanted to go with them, but Gnasher had pulled him up to the registration table.

"Name?" asked the girl behind the table. She was scowling as much as Dennis was, and next to her was a white Tripe Hound. Dennis stared at it, and the girl stared at Gnasher.

"Nice dog!" they both said at the same time.

"This is Gnasher," said Dennis.

"This is Gnarla," said the girl. "She's gonna help me judge this stupid competition. I'd rather be running the coconut shy, but they forced us into it. I'm Dannie."

"Now I get it," said Dennis with a scowl. "GIRLS! Ok Gnasher, if you wanna impress Gnarla, you can enter the contest. Just don't go softy on me!"

Gnasher gave a menacing little growl.

The first event was a dog race. There were four dogs entered – Gnasher, Foo-Foo (covered in ribbons), Spotty Perkins's Pekinese, Sweetums, and Bertie Blenkinsop's sausage dog, Twinkle.

"Think you can beat them?" chuckled Dennis.

"Gnash!" barked Gnasher. He could see that Gnarla was watching and he was looking forward to showing off his speed and strength.

The dogs stood at one end of the track and the owners stood at the other, holding out their dog's favourite food. Walter held out a limp piece of lettuce. Spotty and

Bertie held out fairy cakes. Dennis held out a string of sausages. Dannie stood next to the dogs and held up her starter pistol. She looked even more furious than before.

"GO!" she yelled, firing the pistol. Foo-Foo skipped forward. Twinkle was so scared by the noise and the sight of the sausages that she ran straight up a passing gent's trouser leg. Sweetums hid his face behind his paws and sat yelping pitifully. Gnasher gave a loud bark and ran after Foo-Foo, leapfrogged over his back and reached the finish line first!

"The Tripe Hound wins the first contest!" announced Dannie.

"It's a fix!" sobbed Walter. "Cheat!"

"I saw no cheating, you softy," snapped Dannie. "Come on, I wanna get this over with. Next event – the agility trials!"

The agility course had been set up in another corner of the big top. There were jumps, tunnels to run through, hoops to leap through and seesaws to balance on. Dennis rubbed his hands together.

"This'll be easy for you, Gnasher, with all the escaping we've had to do!"

Gnarla was watching carefully. Gnasher puffed out his chest and took his place at the starting line. Dennis sat down and munched on one of Gnasher's sausages.

"You're supposed to run around the course with him, you know," simpered Walter. "Don't you know anything about showing dogs?"

"Gnasher doesn't need anyone to show him what to do," chortled Dennis. **"He's not a softy dog!"**

Dannie fired the starting pistol and Gnasher sailed over the first jump. He shot through the tunnel and balanced easily on the seesaw. He somersaulted through the air and tumbled through three hoops.

"Easy," thought Gnasher as he strolled back to the starting line. He hoped Gnarla was watching.

Foo-Foo was next, but he had got an attack of nerves. Walter was trying to encourage him.

"Don't be afraid, Foo-Foo darling," he whispered. "I know it's scary, but it will all be over soon!"

"What's scary about it?" scoffed Dennis. His grin widened as he had one of his brilliant ideas "I know, Gnasher will go round with him and show him how to do it!"

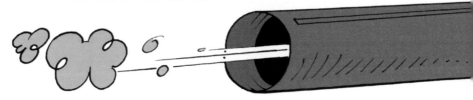

"No!" trembled Walter, but it was too late. Gnasher gave Foo-Foo a little nip on the tail to get him started and Foo-Foo sprang into the air and smashed into the first jump. The poles crashed to the ground and Foo-Foo landed on them in a heap.

"*YOWWL!*" cried Foo-Foo.

"**Gnash! Get up!**" Gnasher ordered. "**Keep going!**"

"Get on with it!" growled Dannie.

Foo-Foo ran towards the plastic tunnel but stopped suddenly at the entrance, quivering.

"*Poor Foo-Foo doesn't like tunnels!*" cried Walter, running after him. But before he could get there, Gnasher headbutted Foo-Foo's bottom. With a yelp Foo-Foo dived into the tunnel. Gnasher jumped on top of it and chased Foo-Foo out by squashing it. By this time Foo-Foo was panting, his ribbons were coming loose and his hair was getting frizzy.

"What are you doing to my poor Foo-Foo?" squeaked Walter. Foo-Foo tore around the course, sending jumps and tests flying in all directions.

"He's helping him finish the course!"

guffawed Dennis as Foo-Foo tried to balance on the seesaw. Finally Gnasher jumped on the other end of it and the two dogs seesawed up and down so fast that Foo-Foo went green and the seesaw came off its base!

"He's finished the course all right," grinned Dannie,

looking at the wrecked agility trial.
"It's fine by me! If it's broken, the
other two can't finish it! Next – the
obedience trials!"

Sweetums and
Twinkle heaved
sighs of relief.

"Foo-Foo will
sail through this!"
boasted Walter.
"He's the most
obedient dog in
Beanotown!"

Dennis
looked at the
chaos Gnasher had
created so far and grinned.

"I thought this was gonna be a softy trial," he chortled, "but it's ended up being the best menace of the week!"

For the obedience trials the dogs had to sit in front of a large bowl of their favourite food, but not touch it until their owners said so. While they waited they had to perform tricks.

"Pirouette on the spot, Foo-Foo!" called Walter. Foo-Foo stood up on his spindly back legs and did a little pirouette.

"Roly poly!" called Bertie. Twinkle tried to do a roly poly but just ended up tying herself into a tangled knot.

"Balance a ball on your nose!" called Bertie. But the ball was as big as Sweetums and he was squashed under it!

"I don't reckon you can get a tripe

hound to balance a ball on his nose or do a pirouette!" chortled Dannie.

"The trick is," Dennis told Dannie, "to ask your Tripe Hound to do something he wants to do! Gnasher – menace 'em!"

Gnasher leapt into action! He nibbled Foo-Foo's kneecaps and gnashed Walter's ankles. He headed Sweetums's ball into Twinkle's stomach and unknotted her.

"Stop!" shrieked Walter. "This isn't how you run a dog show!"

Gnasher ran after the ball to show Gnarla his footballing skills. He kicked it to Dennis, who dribbled it past the wrecked agility course. Dennis weaved between Dannie and Gnarla and flicked the ball back to Gnasher, who gave it a powerful header... straight into the central support of the big top!

The support creaked.

It started to lean sideways.

The big top trembled... swayed... and...

CRASH!

The whole canopy collapsed around them!

There were shouts, screams and whimpers from the three softies and their dogs.

There were guffaws and barks from Dennis, Gnasher, Dannie and Gnarla.

They all clambered out of the end of the tent. The softies staggered away with their dogs as Dannie handed Dennis a huge red rosette.

"I declare you the winner of the Most Menacing Dog Show Ever!" she chortled.

Gnarla gave Gnasher a wink.
"Next stop Grrrufts!" she barked.
"See you at next year's carnival!"

MOUNTAINTOP MENACE

It was amazing. It was a miracle. Dad had entered a competition and actually WON it! He had come first in a spot-the-difference competition and the first prize was a family skiing holiday.

"The first time EVER!" whooped Dad, punching the air with his fist. "I'm a winner!"

"You're a right nutter," Dennis corrected. "You've never been skiing in your life! I can't wait to see this!"

Dad's eyes narrowed. "And what makes you think you'll be seeing anything?" he asked. "I haven't forgotten our last holiday, you pest.

"We don't want to get banned from anywhere else!"

Dennis folded his arms, lowered his eyebrows and stuck out his bottom lip.

"I want to come too!" he growled.

"Dad and I needed a holiday when we came back from the last one!" twittered Mum. "I want a nice relaxing break!"

"We'll get someone to come and look after you for the week," Dad went on.

"Perhaps the Colonel...?" Mum put in.

"Huh, I don't need anyone to look after me," Dennis argued. "Anyway, I wanna come! And you won't get anyone to look after me."

He was right. Troops of possible Dennis-sitters came, met Dennis and left at top speed. Not one of them lasted longer than ten minutes. Finally Mum and Dad were forced to take Dennis with them.

"But there must be no peashooters!" warned Dad.

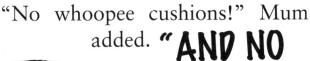

"No whoopee cushions!" Mum added. **"AND NO MENACING!"**

they said together. "Or you'll be on the first plane home!"

Dennis just grinned. He was looking forward to seeing Mum and Dad on skis.

"Skiing's for softies," he told Gnasher. "I'm gonna be a snowboarder!"

Mum, Dad, Bea and Dennis flew to the ski resort in a small plane. The captain of the plane had only ever met nice, well-behaved little boys. He didn't know about menaces. So he asked if Dennis would like to go into the cockpit and see all the controls. Mum and Dad tried to tell the captain it was a bad idea.

"You'll regret it," Mum said.

"And we want to arrive in one piece," added Dad.

But he just smiled and thought they were joking. So Dennis went into the cockpit. Mum and Dad crossed their fingers and hid behind their magazines.

The captain stayed calm when Dennis blew a very loud raspberry at air traffic control over the radio. Pilots are trained to deal with all sorts of emergencies.

He bit his lip very hard when Dennis pressed a big red button and oxygen masks dropped onto all the passengers' heads. But he still didn't lose his cool.

It was only when Dennis leaned against the controls and nearly crashed the plane into a mountain that the captain changed his mind. He pulled at the controls and the plane rose steeply, just missing the mountaintop.

"Get back to your seat!" he bellowed as soon as he had swerved around the mountain. Sweat was dripping down his forehead. "And don't move until we land!"

The captain was carried away on
a stretcher, gibbering. In all his years
of pilot training he had never been
prepared for anything like Dennis.

"I tried to warn him," sighed
Mum wearily.

The ski resort was covered in
snow and the sun was shining. The
sky was blue.

"How lovely," said Mum as they
looked around their chalet. When
they walked into the sitting room

they met the family they would have to share it with. Dennis groaned. Standing in between his parents was the softiest softy he had ever seen (apart from Walter, of course).

"We're Mr and Mrs Finch-Salmon, and this is our son Cedric," said the man. Dad and Mr Finch-Salmon shook hands and started talking about the weather. Cedric walked up to Dennis with a horrible smirk on his face. His nose was stuck up in the air.

"I am an excellent skier," he drawled.

"I have been skiing since I was a toddler. I can ski backwards. Have you ever been skiing?"

101

Dennis looked him up and down. Cedric was wearing a bow tie and his legs were slightly bandy. "Nah," Dennis shrugged. "But it can't be that difficult if you can do it. Anyway, I'm not going to be skiing, only snowboarding"

Cedric stuck his nose even higher in the air.

"Daddy says snowboarding is common," he said. "I suppose it will suit YOU."

"Oh yeah?" rumbled Dennis, clenching his fists. "Listen here, softy features..."

"DENNIS!" snapped Dad, clamping his hand down on Dennis's shoulder. "I want you to make friends with this nice young man."

"How do you do, sir," simpered Cedric. Dennis scowled at him.

Anyone who could suck up to parents like that could do anything! As soon as Dad walked away, Cedric leaned towards him with a smirk.

"Watching you trying to move along on the snow will be a good laugh. You'll spend most of the week upside down in snowdrifts! Haw haw!"

"Grrr, I'll wipe that smile off your face with my snowboard!" growled Dennis through gritted teeth. Cedric smirked again and then let out a false wail.

"Daddy! This nasty boy threatened me!"

"What?" snorted Mr Finch-Salmon.

"Dennis! **BED!**" roared Dad. Dennis stomped off to the bathroom with his hands in his pockets. Perhaps this holiday wasn't such a good thing after all!

When Dennis came out of the bathroom, Cedric was standing there with his towel. He screwed up his face in disgust when he saw Dennis.

"Ugh," sneered Cedric. "How dirty you are. Aren't you going to have an evening bath? I have one every morning and evening."

"Weirdo," muttered Dennis. Then he remembered something. His hand reached into his pocket and a menacing grin spread across his face.

Mum and Dad had said no peashooters and no whoopee cushions, but they hadn't mentioned anything else. Dennis ducked back inside the bathroom and quickly put the soap into his pocket. Then he replaced it with the trick soap he had borrowed from Curly.

"Bathroom's all yours," he told Cedric.

104

Dennis went to his room and waited. He heard the bath water running and he heard Cedric splashing. Then he heard the bath water drain away. Dennis sniggered and whispered to himself, "Five, four, three, two, one…"

"EEEEEK!" There was a piercing scream from the bathroom! "Mummy! Daddy!"

Dennis ran into the corridor just in time. Cedric was standing in the doorway of the bathroom in his pyjamas. He was yelling at the top of his reedy voice. He was completely blue and glowing!

105

"Good one, Curly!"

thought Dennis.

"This is your fault, you menace!"
thundered Mr Finch-Salmon.

"What on earth have you done to my little Cedricy Wedricy?" cried Mrs Finch-Salmon.

Dennis just chortled, then dived back into his room as he saw Mum coming towards him. He didn't want to be sent home just yet!

Next morning, Dennis, Bea, Mum and Dad went to be fitted for skis and snowboards. Then they met their instructor. He took them to the top of a little slope.

"This is called a nursery slope," he said cheerfully. "It's where you will learn to ski before you're allowed on the big slopes."

Just then, Dennis saw Cedric ski past at top speed. (He still had a faint blue tinge.)

"You'll be on the nursery slope all week!" Cedric called out as he went by.

"Oh yeah?" said Dennis. "You don't know the powers of the Menace! I'm not staying on a soppy nursery slope!"

He strapped himself onto his snowboard, pointed it down the mountain and set off after Cedric. After all his skateboarding through the streets of Beanotown, snowboarding was easy!

WHOOSH!

"Woohoo!" whooped Dennis as he powered down the slope, slicing through the white powdery snow. **"Awesome!"**

At the bottom of the slope he skidded to a halt and grinned. This holiday was gonna be a blast!

Dennis took the ski lift back up to the top of the mountain and whizzed down again, even faster this time. He practised a few jumps and swivels then jumped on the lift again.

Meanwhile, on the nursery slope, Dad had just fallen on his bottom for the nineteenth time. Mum was headfirst in a snowdrift.

"I think we're ready for our first proper ski!" bubbled the cheerful ski instructor. He and Dad pulled Mum out of the snowdrift and the beginners' class set off. They got on the same lift as Dennis and arrived at the top of the mountain at the same time.

The beginners started to wind their way slowly down the slope and Dennis chortled as he watched Dad trying to keep his balance. Then he spotted Cedric halfway down.

"I'll show that softy how menaces get down a mountain!" chuckled Dennis. He pushed off and sped down the mountain, but the beginners' class was taking up the whole slope!

"GANGWAY!"

bellowed Dennis as he plunged through the class, scattering new skiers right and left. Dad lost control of his skis and swerved off towards a large tree. Mum landed in another snowdrift. Bea did a jump on her baby snowboard and spun in the air as Dennis whizzed below her. Dennis was pleased with his little sister – she found snowboarding as easy as he did!

"You rascal!" hollered the ski instructor as he rounded up his scattered class. But Dennis was past! As he caught Cedric up, he pulled his catapult from his pocket and aimed a snowball at Cedric's backside. POW!

"YOWEE!"

Cedric clutched his bottom, dropped his ski poles and overbalanced, landing on his back in a snowy ditch and staring up at Dennis's grinning face.

"Did you lose your balance?" Dennis chuckled. "I can see you don't know everything about skiing after all!"

Dennis boarded on down the next slope and saw a group of softies wearing padded ski suits in pretty pastel colours, learning how to stop if they were going too fast.

"Huh, they need to learn how to go fast!" chuckled Dennis. "I'll give them a hand!" He sliced through the snow, weaving towards the softies. One of them turned and saw him. "EEEEEEEEEK!" he shouted. "Ski away! Ski away!"

The whole group sped away from Dennis, whimpering, but they weren't fast enough!

"Make way!" roared Dennis as he crashed into seven softies at the same time. They clung to each

other's waists to stop from falling
and snaked down the slope in a
trembling line, getting faster and
faster. As Dennis curved around
them, the softy in front panicked,
changed direction and led all the
others off the slope and into a heap
in the snow.

At the bottom of the mountain,
back on the nursery slope, Dennis
unstrapped himself from his board
and saw Bea speeding towards him.
She stopped next to him and they
watched as Dad arrived at the
bottom of the mountain.

"Snowman!" Bea
giggled as she pointed
at Dad, who had
pulled himself out of
the snow but was
still white all over.

"You've given me an idea, Bea!" chortled Dennis. "With all this snow, we should have some fun!"

Dennis and Bea made snow-monsters.

Lots of snow-monsters!

Huge, scary snow-monsters!

Ten minutes later, as the beginners and the softies snaked slowly down the nursery slope, they were horrified to see their path blocked by ten enormous white monsters!

"Yikes! It's the Yeti!" screamed the first softy.

"I can't stop!" yelled Mum.

"What a mega menace!" grinned Dennis as the softies and the beginners crashed into the huge snow-monsters he and Bea had built. Snow heads rolled in all directions. People were sticking halfway through the snow bodies. It was chaos! The ski instructor spotted Dennis and shook his fist.

Dennis used the ski lift to the very top of the steepest slope. He stood at the top and looked out over the mountain range. The sky was blue. The sun beat down. Dennis let out a whoop of menacing delight. The only thing that was missing was someone to race against! Then Dennis had one of his brilliant ideas. He quickly made a large snowball and positioned it on the edge of the slope. He would race the snowball to the bottom!

Dennis pointed his board down the mountain and pushed off, flicking the snowball at the same time. He scooted away, just ahead of the tumbling snowball! But as they got further down the slope, the snowball collected more and more snow. It got bigger and bigger! Dennis went even faster, with the enormous snowball close behind him. Just in time he reached the bottom and darted out of the way.

The beginners and the softies had just escaped from the snow-monsters when...

WHUMP!

The massive snowball hit them and tumbled them down again. Dennis roared with laughter.

But Dad had seen everything. He marched towards Dennis with the ski instructor. They were both covered in snow and looked furious. Dennis gave them a cheerful wave and jumped onto the ski lift just in time. He was carried away before they could reach him!

Then Dennis saw the ski instructor talking to the ski lift operator. Just as the ski lift was above deep snow, it stopped. Dennis dangled above, his fists clenched in fury.

"Let me down!" he bellowed. The ski instructor folded his arms and laughed.

"You'll stay up there until you've learned your lesson!" he shouted.

"And until we've had a nice, unmenaced ski!" added Dad.

Dennis watched in a rage as the beginners got onto the drag lifts and were carried back up to the top of the easiest slope. Then he looked down and a grin spread slowly across his face. Snowboarding was just like skateboarding – and he had done bigger jumps than this on a skateboard!

"Bombs away!" bellowed Dennis as he slipped out of the lift and dropped skilfully through the air to land on the soft snow. He sped down to catch the beginners, who were still on the drag lifts.

Dennis boarded past them, but his board was tipped at such an angle that he sprayed snow into their faces.

"Argghh!" yelled one.

"I can't see!" cried another.

One by one they lost their grip on the ski lift and fell like dominoes into the heavy snow.

As they rose up they looked like abominable snowmen!

"You... you..." spluttered the ski instructor, as Dennis whizzed past him.

"See you back at the chalet!" bellowed Dennis to Mum and Dad as they pulled themselves out of the snow. He whizzed to the foot of the mountain, unstrapped the board and tramped back to the chalet. No one was there.

Cedric was still stuck in a snowdrift. Everyone else was struggling to escape from the trail of chaos Dennis had left behind him.

Dennis grabbed a fistful of comics and a huge mug of hot chocolate, and settled down in the armchair beside the roaring fire.

"Now this is my idea of a relaxing holiday!" he chortled as he opened the first comic!

DENNIS THE DETECTIVE

It was just another boring day at Beanotown School.

Elastic bands whizzed across the hallways.

The school caretaker ducked and weaved as he made his way through the school, avoiding small missiles and pointed paper aeroplanes. Now and then he shook his fist at the classroom doors.

In the sick room the nurse was trying to deal with everything from nose bleeds to stink bomb allergies (not to mention paperclips in ears and one small boy with a strawberry up his left nostril). And most of her patients were there because of Dennis.

Dennis himself was even more bored than usual. He had tried to get out of the window but, after his exciting escape the previous week, all the classroom windows had been nailed shut. This was making everyone even more bad tempered than usual, because it was a hot day and there was no air. Everything smelled like stink bombs.

In the front row, all the softies were busily getting on with their work. At least, almost all the softies were. Walter and Spotty were starting on their Maths homework, but Bertie kept pausing in his algebra to stare into space.

Dennis let out a long sigh and absentmindedly aimed a paper aeroplane at the back of Walter's head. There was only one thing for it. He was going to have to make an escape plan. He glanced over at Curly and Pie Face. Curly was asleep and drooling on his Maths book. Pie Face was doodling pies all over his textbook. At Dennis's feet, Gnasher was gnawing on Walter the softy's favourite teddy. Dennis needed a distraction if he was going to escape, but it didn't look as if his menacing friends were gonna help him at all.

Just then Walter let out a loud wail.

"What's the matter, Walter dear?" asked Mr Hodges.

"My glasses are missing!" sobbed Walter. "I put them down for a moment to put some eye drops in my eyes and now they're gone!"

The classroom was in uproar. It was the perfect moment for Dennis to slip away. He winked at Gnasher and got ready to go and do a bit of menacing, when suddenly...

"DENNIS!" bellowed Mr Hodges. "Where are those glasses?"

Dennis folded his arms and scowled at Mr Hodges.

"I don't know!" Dennis growled. "What would I want with 'em?"

Mr Hodges clenched his fists and crumbled his piece of chalk into dust.

"I will not allow my favourite pupil to be upset!" he roared. "Where are those glasses, you menace?"

Before Dennis could reply, Gnasher sprang into action. He aimed at the seat of Mr Hodges's trousers and bit down hard.

"**YOWEE!**" shrieked Mr Hodges, clutching his bottom.

"Let's go, Gnasher!" called Dennis, and they raced out of the room before Mr Hodges could stop them.

Dennis and Gnasher raced down the corridor and skidded around the caretaker (who dropped his bucket of mop water for the fifteenth time that day). They shot out of the school and into the playground, where Mr Pump was taking a football lesson.

Dennis raced over the touchline, weaved around the winger and hurtled towards the striker, who had just been passed the ball. Dennis steamed past him, stole the ball and charged towards the goalkeeper, whose knees began to knock. Dribbling around three petrified defenders, Dennis flicked the ball into the air and, performing a perfect overhead scissor kick, he powered the ball straight past the goalkeeper's ear and slammed it into the back of the net.

As Mr Pump yelled **"GOAL!"** Dennis and Gnasher shot out of the school gates and disappeared up the road in a cloud of dust.

"Why would I take Walter's softy glasses?" Dennis raged to Gnasher when they were safely away from school. "I've done better menaces than that in my sleep!"

He started filling water bombs to throw at Minnie while he talked (there was no point in wasting menacing time).

"GNASH!" Gnasher agreed, wondering if it was time for tea yet.

"I can't let people think I'd do such a stupid menace!" Dennis went on. "There's only one thing for it. I'll have to find out who did take the stupid glasses! And that's gonna cut into my menacing time."

Just then, Minnie appeared at the corner and a grin spread slowly over Dennis's face. Three water bombs whizzed through the air and

burst on Minnie's head. " **G - r - r - r !** **You -** " she bellowed, pulling out a catapult. But Dennis had already gone!

Dennis raced home to his garage, which was packed to the roof with boxes full of old menacing equipment. Dennis rummaged around and found all sorts of old treasures... his very first catapult, his water-squirting dummy, his jet-propelled pushchair and even Gnasher's first dog basket, which was almost chewed to pieces.

At last, after emptying about half the boxes, Dennis found what he was looking for.

"My magnifying glass!" he grinned. He held it up and peered into the corner at an especially large spider. "This is gonna help me find clues," Dennis told Gnasher. He pocketed the spider (always the quickest way to cause a distraction) and sprinted out of the garage just as Mum walked in.

Mum was looking for her super-large pack of industrial-strength cleaner. Bea had found a tin of orange paint and redecorated the kitchen. But when she saw all the empty boxes, Mum staggered and forgot all about the orange paint. The entire garage was filled with menacing equipment she thought she would never have to see again.

Mum's mouth opened and closed silently. The car was completely buried under a mountain of water pistols. Old catapults dangled from the light and burst whoopee cushions fluttered in the air.

"Dennis!" said Mum through gritted teeth. Then she fainted backwards into a pile of Gnasher's old dog biscuits.

"I've gotta find some clues," Dennis told Gnasher as they raced into Beanotown. "Those glasses are hiding somewhere and I'm gonna find them! So I've gotta think like a detective – and what's the first thing that all detectives do?"

"Gnash?" asked Gnasher. He was hoping that whatever it was involved sausages.

"Return to the crime scene!" said Dennis. "Come on, let's go!"

They dashed up to the school just as the last teacher screeched out of the school gates in his car. Dennis examined every inch of the classroom through his magnifying glass. He emptied all the drawers, turned all the desks upside down, checked inside every cupboard and peered behind every shelf.

He found a couple of old water

pistols, six sweets covered in fluff, a love letter from Walter to his girlfriend Matilda (Dennis dropped it quickly and wiped his hands on his jumper in disgust) and five beetles living in Plug's old pencil case. Then, underneath Billy Whizz's chair, Dennis found his first proper clue. It was the cloth from inside a glasses case.

"Aha!" Dennis exclaimed, peering at the cloth through his magnifying glass. In the corner, embroidered in pink thread, was the name 'Walter'. Next, Dennis glimpsed a pink ribbon on the floor under Minnie's desk. It was the ribbon Walter used to hang his glasses around his neck.

"Another clue!" Dennis said. "It's gotta be either Minnie or Billy!"

Dennis raced out of the classroom and past the caretaker, who tried to grab him. But he slipped on the wet floor and landed with a BUMP in the mop bucket.

"Come back here!" he bellowed, trying to drag the bucket off his bottom and chase Dennis at the same time.

"Not likely!" chortled Dennis. He charged back out of school and down to the high street, just in time to see Minnie disappearing into the joke shop.

Dennis darted into the shop and hid behind a display of fake blood at the back of the shop. Minnie was looking through the scary masks and he watched her carefully. Her pockets had all sorts of bulges in them. Dennis could see a catapult-shaped bulge, a tennis-ball-shaped bulge and a mousetrap-shaped bulge, but no bulges that looked like glasses. If she had them, they must be in her rucksack.

As Minnie paid for a werewolf mask, Dennis got ready for a spot of menacing detective work. When Minnie walked out of the shop, Dennis made a flying leap through the air and grabbed her rucksack.

"OY!" screeched Minnie. "What are you playing at, Dennis?"

"You're the Great Beanotown Glasses Grabber!" Dennis bellowed, tugging the rucksack towards him.

"What would I want with that softy's glasses?"

Minnie roared, tugging the rucksack back towards her. Dennis held on to it so hard that the bag ripped in two, the contents flew into the air and Dennis and Minnie tumbled backwards. Dennis hit the fake blood display and Minnie crashed into the stink-bomb stand. Dennis looked at the contents of Minnie's bag as they zoomed over his head and hit the shopkeeper on the nose. The glasses weren't there! Dennis pulled a peg from his pocket, clipped it on his nose and burst out of the door with Minnie and Gnasher close behind him. Fake blood poured out of the door, over the step and onto the pavement.

"Help!" screamed Mrs Perkins (Spotty's mum), who was just passing the shop. She saw the fake blood and keeled over backwards.

"What's that stench?" squealed Gertrude Blenkinsop (Bertie's sister), clutching her nose and tripping over her high heels. Minnie glared at Dennis, her fists clenched. She had landed on a pile of the stink bombs and she smelled very bad indeed.

"This means I'm gonna have to take a bath!" Minnie fumed. "And I've already had one this month!"

"Want to borrow a peg?" asked Dennis with a grin.

"Come back here!" bellowed the shopkeeper.

"OY! You!" shouted a familiar voice. Sergeant Slipper was pounding up the road towards them. Dennis sprang to his feet and Gnasher gave himself a good shake, spraying fake blood in all directions.

Then Dennis grabbed
his skateboard and
whizzed around
the corner before
Sergeant Slipper
had chance
to blink.

Dennis headed
over to Billy's house.
The glasses cloth had been
under Billy's chair – he
must have the glasses. But
Billy was not going to be as easy
to catch as Minnie.

"We've gotta think of a plan to trap him," Dennis told Gnasher. They stopped outside Billy's house and Dennis drew a roll of tennis net from his back pocket.

"I knew this would come in useful!" he grinned. He strung the net across Billy's front door and rang the doorbell. It opened at once and a figure shot out, got tangled in the net and landed in a heap at Dennis's feet. Dennis whipped out his water pistol and blasted them with jets of water.

"**ARRGGHH!**" roared the captive, struggling to stand up. It wasn't Billy – it was his Mum – going out for her afternoon jog!

"Where's Billy?" fumed Dennis.

At that moment a blur whizzed past them in a cloud of dust.

"**GNASHER!**" yelled Dennis,

jumping on his skateboard. Gnasher leaped out from behind a bush as Billy zoomed down the path, skidded between his legs and tripped him up.

CRASH!

Dennis powered over Billy and Gnasher and screeched to a stop. He jumped off his skateboard, grabbed Billy and held on tight.

"Where are they?" he growled.

"Where are what?" asked Billy. "And why did you squirt my mum with a water pistol?"

"If I don't find that softy's glasses, I'm gonna be accused of a completely stupid menace!" Dennis raged. "You're my number-one suspect and I'm not gonna let the whole of Beanotown think I took them!"

"Well I didn't take them!" said Billy. "What would I want with them? If I wore glasses they'd have to be made of super-strong material to cope with my speed!"

"Turn out your pockets!" Dennis ordered.

Billy shoved his hands in his pockets and pulled out a yoyo, a ball of string, a couple of melted chocolate mini eggs left over from

Easter and a small dormouse. But there were no glasses.

"You were my only suspect," groaned Dennis. "If you don't have them, who does?"

"Not my problem!" grinned Billy, shaking himself free of Dennis's grip. He zoomed off into the distance. Dennis frowned so hard his eyebrows knitted together.

"This is turning into a bad day," he told Gnasher. "I haven't had time to do any menacing at all."

"GNASH!" agreed Gnasher. It had been a bad day for sausages as well.

Just then they saw someone walking slowly along on the other side of the road, feeling their way and using the garden walls as a guide.

"There's just one more suspect to try," said Dennis as a menacing gleam shone in his eyes. "Walter the softy himself!"

Gnasher looked doubtful.

"It's a long shot," said Dennis. "But we might pick up a few more clues... and have a bit of fun along the way!"

Dennis and Gnasher followed Walter along the street to Matilda's house. Walter knocked on the door and Matilda answered it.

"Oh, Matilda-wilda," said Walter with a softy blush. "I picked you some flowers. They're almost as pretty as you!"

"Oh!" simpered Matilda in delight. Then her smile changed to a scowl. "What are those? You think I look like a weed?!"

Walter was holding a bunch of ragged nettles and dandelions!

"Oh, if only I had my glasses!" Walter wailed.

Dennis snorted with laughter as Matilda slammed the door in Walter's face.

Walter walked on down the street, unaware that Dennis was close behind him.

Dennis could see someone coming towards Walter. They were walking in a very strange way – weaving and swerving all over the pavement, just like Walter.

"Has someone else had their glasses grabbed?" wondered Dennis. But then he saw that it was Bertie Blenkinsop, and he was wearing a big pair of glasses.

Walter blundered sideways, bumped into a dustbin and apologised to it. Bertie put his arms out in front of him, clutched at a tree and tried to shake hands with it.

"Hmmm," said Dennis. "Come to think of it, I've never seen Bertie wearing glasses before!"

At that moment, SMACK! Bertie and Walter walked into each other and fell down, clutching their noses and wailing.

Dennis strode over to them. He grabbed the glasses from Bertie's face and shoved them on Walter's nose. Walter stopped sobbing, peered through them and squealed in excitement.

"My glasses! My lovely glasses!"

Dennis could hardly believe it. Had Bertie gone potty?

"Are you trying to turn into a menace?" Dennis asked Bertie in amazement.

"No!" sobbed Bertie. "But I want to be like Walter so much! When I saw his glasses lying on the table, I couldn't resist! I thought he had a spare pair! I threw the ribbon and the cloth away – I'm sorry, Walter!"

"Oh Bertie," gushed Walter, "I quite understand! Of course you would want to look like me!"

"UGGHH! Stop it!" roared Dennis. He was starting to feel sick. "I've missed out on a whole day's menacing just to prove I didn't take Walter's softy glasses! You're gonna tell everyone in school that you took them!"

"Oh, I can't!" sobbed Bertie, his knees quivering. "Mr Hodges will tell me off! He might give me detention! I couldn't bear the shame!"

"It's all right, Bertie," said Walter

154

pompously. "Dennis can take the blame... he's used to it."

"Oh yeah?" growled Dennis. He pushed his face up so close to Walter's that their noses were almost touching. The sweet, perfumed smell of Walter made Dennis's nose twitch in horror.

"If I keep quiet about Bertie grabbing your glasses, after all the menacing time I lost today, I want something in return!"

"Wh... what do you want?" asked Walter, his knees trembling.

"An ice cream a day for a month," said Dennis. "And a big juicy bone for Gnasher every other day!"

"Anything to save Bertie from the shame of detention!" cried Walter. "Who can blame him for wanting to be more like me?"

"Mental," said Dennis to Gnasher.

155

"Oh Walter, you're my hero!" sighed Bertie.

"Look!" cried Walter, pointing over Dennis's shoulder. Dennis turned around and a grin spread wide across his face.

A huge crowd of people was marching towards him. Minnie was leading the charge, still ponging slightly (even after three baths). The school caretaker was there, still trying to tug the mop bucket off his bottom. The entire school football team was there too, together with Dennis's mum, the joke-shop owner, Mrs Perkins, Gertie Blenkinsop, Sergeant Slipper and Billy's mum.

"Er, maybe it hasn't been such a bad day for menacing after all!" chortled Dennis, leaping onto his skateboard. "Come on, Gnasher. SCARPER!"

MENACE MAN

"Mighty Man is way better than Amazing Man," Curly said, peering over at Pie Face's comic. "Only rubbish superheroes wear capes."

"At least Amazing Man doesn't wear his underpants over his trousers," retorted Pie Face, jabbing a finger at Mighty Man's blue and yellow outfit.

Dennis, Pie Face and Curly were sitting on the bridge reading their comics (in between dropping water bombs on the heads of passers by). Dennis elbowed both of them.

"Shut up!" he said.
"Here comes the Colonel!"

They waited until the Colonel was in position and then dropped three water bombs on him, one after the other.

"Who? What? Where?" spluttered the Colonel. But he could not see the menaces, so he stomped on his way, wringing out his hat and muttering.

159

"Amazing Man has got a stupid fatal weakness," continued Curly, flicking through his comic. "He's got really bad hay fever – that's daft!"

"Yeah, but at least Amazing Man works alone – he doesn't need a wet sidekick like Mighty Man does!" Pie Face argued.

"Shut UP!" grumbled Dennis again. "I'm sick of hearing about those stupid superheroes – and here comes that sap Bertie Blenkinsop!"

The three menaces took careful aim.

WHACK! OOOF! SPLASH!

Their water bombs got Bertie's head, stomach and shoes at the same time. Dennis roared with laughter as Bertie ran home wailing.

"Mighty   Man's

160

arch enemy is way cooler than Amazing Man's arch enemy," Curly went on. Dennis rolled his eyes.

"What do you reckon, Dennis?" asked Pie Face. "Who's the best superhero – Amazing Man or Mighty Man?"

"Huh," said Dennis. "Your softy superheroes are just like Walter in a pair of tights! They're both rubbish!"

"Oh yeah?" said Pie Face. "So which superhero do you think is best?"

"None of them," said Dennis. "A real superhero would be a menacing mastermind who would really scare off the bad guys and show them who was boss!"

"Stop arguing," said Curly suddenly. "Here comes Spotty Perkins – get your water bombs ready!"

When they had run out of water bombs they headed for the skate park to practise their softy-squashing techniques. But all the talk about superheroes had given Dennis an idea.

"You know what Beanotown is missing?" he asked Gnasher as he performed an ollie over the heads of three snivelling softies. "A real baddy-bashing superhero! And I know just the menace for the job!"

"Gnash?" asked Gnasher hopefully. He could see it already – Super-Gnasher! Terror of pampered poodles everywhere!

"No, me!" Dennis exclaimed. "You can be my trusty sidekick! We'll rid Beanotown of everyone who causes trouble – for us!"

Dennis raced home and to Mum's wardrobe. He was sure he had seen just the thing he was looking for in there. He searched through piles of nylon nighties and viscose vests until he found it – a red and black striped cape that Mum had worn for Hallowe'en one year. (She had dressed up as Dennis and scared all the neighbours silly.)

Dennis cut the main part of the cape off until it was just long enough for Gnasher. Then he fastened it around Gnasher's neck. Next, Dennis cut a long, thin strip of material and snipped two eyes holes into it. Then he tied it around his head and grinned at Gnasher. "Menace Man and Danger Dog!" he chortled. "Beanotown's not gonna know what hit it!"

Menace Man pulled out a piece of paper and made a list of arch enemies. It was quite long.

"Humph," said Menace Man. "There's a lot of arch enemies to conquer. Maybe I'll just take the top five today

WALTER
Sgt SLIPPER
the COLONEL
BERTIE
SPOTTY
MINNIE

– we can start on the rest tomorrow."

Dennis loaded up his pockets with superhero equipment, grabbed his Menacemobile and headed for the Beanotown police station, where arch-enemy number one was just creeping up on a couple of unsuspecting menaces.

164

Sergeant Slipper had been having a very good day. He had told nine boys off for playing football too loudly. He had written a long report for the chief constable about why he should be given more holiday time. He had confiscated a yoyo and a catapult from Curly, and he was planning to play with them later. Best of all, he hadn't seen Dennis all day.

And now he was going to catch two menaces! The boys were hiding behind a hedge with peashooters, waiting for Billy to whizz past so they could get in some moving-target practice. Sergeant Slipper crept up behind them, his arms raised ready to catch them. Closer! Closer...

POW! A custard bomb hit the back of his head and he spun around. **SPLAT!** Another custard bomb hit him in the face.

"**Run, menaces!**" yelled Dennis. "I'll take care of him!"

"**It's Menace Man!**" yelled the menaces as they ran in the opposite direction. "**WICKED!**"

"Who did that?" bellowed Sergeant Slipper, wiping globs of custard out of his eyes. When he spotted Dennis his mouth opened very wide – just wide enough for Dennis to aim a third custard bomb into it.

"UMPHUMMBURBLE!" spluttered the amazed Sergeant Slipper.

"I'm here to make sure you leave all menaces alone!" yelled Dennis. "And Danger Dog is here to make sure you learn how to keep fit!"

Dennis chuckled as Gnasher sped towards Sergeant Slipper, his cape flying out behind him. Sergeant Slipper turned and ran as fast as he could back to his comfy police station!

"That's dealt with arch enemy number one," Dennis said, brushing his hands. "Now for arch enemy number two!"

The Colonel was doing what he enjoyed best; he was shouting.

"Outrageous!" he bawled. "Your commanding officer will hear about this!"

Bea, who he was shouting at, blew an enormous raspberry.

"Unbelievable!" hollered the Colonel. "First you crawl through my training grounds and leave sticky handprints all over my best soldiers, and now you blow raspberries at me! Intolerable! We're going to see your parents!"

The Colonel picked Bea up by her nappy. She squirmed and struggled, but she couldn't quite get free. Just then...

KERPOW! A stink bomb burst at the Colonel's feet.

PWANG! A dried pea shot the pin that held Bea's nappy and opened it. Bea dropped to the ground and started to crawl away, but stopped in amazement when she saw who held the peashooter.

"Scarper Bea!" cried Menace Man. "He's not going anywhere!"

Bea darted through a hole in the garden fence and escaped. Dennis clasped a peg onto his nose as the Colonel pointed at him in astonishment.

"Who...?

What...?"

But the combination of the stink bomb and Bea's nappy was too much for him – he went green and keeled over backwards.

"Germ warfare!" he gasped as he fainted.

Walter the softy was having a doll's tea party with his two dearest chums, Bertie and Spotty.

"More tea, Fluffy Bunny?" asked

Spotty, pouring out a cup of watery tea for his favourite soft toy.

"Would you like a butterfly cake, Jemima?" Bertie asked his little doll.

"Who would like to sing a happy song about flowers with me?" simpered Walter.

The three softies had just started to sing when **SMASH!** A stink bomb landed in the middle of their tea party table!

"Hold it!" bellowed a menacing voice. "No softy singing allowed!"

Dennis dropped down from the tree where he had been hiding and Gnasher landed beside him, his cape acting as a parachute.

"Save me!" wailed Spotty, diving under the table. The dolls and teddies were flung into the bushes around them.

"E-E-E-E-E-EEK!" screeched Bertie, throwing the teapot into the air in terror. Walter tried to catch it but he missed and it landed on his foot.

"WAHH-H!" cried Walter, hopping around and clutching his throbbing toe.

"Menace Man is here to save the day!" Dennis declared. "The streets of Beanotown will be free from softy tea parties!"

"The smell!" wailed Walter. "I can't bear the smell!"

The three softies fled, holding their noses and calling for their mumsies. Gnasher quickly dug a hole, then buried all the dolls and teddies. Dennis helped him flatten down the earth.

"A good day's work, Danger Dog!" said Menace Man. "We've conquered our first five arch-enemies! This calls for a sausage feast!"

Dennis and Gnasher raced towards the butcher's shop, but suddenly Dennis was running alone. He swirled around and glowered through his red-and-black mask. Someone had caught Gnasher by his cape. It was Dad!

"You can't capture a superhero!" Dennis growled.

"Every superhero has an evil rival!" said Dad. "I've been hearing all sorts of stories about a masked menace! You're coming home and going to your room!"

"You can't send a superhero to his room!" fumed Dennis.

"Your sidekick is now in my power! You have no choice!"

Dad held the struggling Gnasher in a tight grip and marched off. Dennis followed him back home and saw Mum in the doorway with her arms folded.

"So that's where my cape went!" she exclaimed when she saw Gnasher and Dennis. "I've had to spend all morning tidying up my wardrobe!"

"Right," said Dad, heading upstairs. "Gnasher's going to be locked in your room!"

"Where Danger Dog goes, I go!" Dennis growled, stomping up the stairs behind Dad. Soon they were stuck in the bedroom.

"TRAPPED!" said Dennis. "But that doesn't mean they've won. You can't keep a menacing superhero down!"

Dennis opened his wardrobe and a pile of menacing equipment fell out.

"My emergency stash!" Dennis grinned, opening the window. Soon the windowsill was bristling with catapults, rubber arrows, peashooters and lots of water-bomb launchers.

"Now all I need is an arch enemy!" Dennis told Gnasher. He didn't have to wait long.

Minnie was caught in a hail of small missiles – Dennis used one peashooter while he reloaded another with lightning speed.

Billy slipped on a banana skin that Dennis catapulted onto the path ahead of him.

Walter's girlfriend Matilda had her new hairstyle ruined by a carefully aimed paintball.

Dennis was just refreshing his stink bomb supply, ready for the next passer by, when he noticed something unusual. Over at the Colonel's house, someone was climbing out of a window – and it wasn't the Colonel. Dennis grabbed his binoculars and trained them on the man. He was carrying a large sack and his pockets were bulging. Dennis could just see a glint of gold. He focused his binoculars on the pockets. Then he grabbed his bow and rubber arrows.

"This is a job for Menace Man!" he roared. He took aim, fired and... THUNK! The rubber arrow landed right in the middle of the burglar's forehead! The shock made him lose his balance and he toppled out of the window into the Colonel's begonias.

"Come on, Danger Dog!" Dennis yelled. He climbed onto the windowsill and shimmied down the drainpipe, while Gnasher again used his cape as a parachute and floated down to the ground. They raced over to where the burglar was just crawling out of the begonias, with leaves sticking out of his ears.

"Gotcha!" Dennis yelled. He sprang into the air and landed on top of the burglar.

"**O-O-O-OF!**" gasped the burglar as Dennis flattened him. The sack fell open to reveal all the Colonel's favourite toy soldiers. But Dennis was looking at the gold coins pouring out of the burglar's pockets.

"Danger Dog, you know what to do!" he ordered.

Gnasher raced off and returned after a few minutes, dragging Sergeant Slipper by the ankles of his trousers. When Sergeant Slipper saw the burglar, he got very excited.

"You're going behind bars!" he roared.

"Anything!" gasped the burglar. "Anything! Just get this menace off me!"

"Splendid show, old boy!" exclaimed the Colonel when he found his toy soldiers were safe. "Deserve a medal!"

"The local paper wants to interview you!" gasped Mum in delight. "My son the hero!"

"Not bad, not bad at all," agreed Dad.

Bea just blew an enormous raspberry.

Dennis and Gnasher went to meet Curly and Pie Face in the skate park.

"Never thought I'd see you as the local hero," sniggered Curly.

"Didn't think you cared about the Colonel's soldiers that much," added Pie Face with a smirk.

"I don't care about his soldiers," snorted Dennis. "But I do care about his health!"

"Eh?" asked Curly and Pie Face.

"The burglar's pockets were full of gold!" Dennis grinned. He emptied his pockets and piled gold coins onto his skateboard. "Chocolate gold!"

"Wicked!" gasped Pie Face, letting the chocolate coins run through his fingers.

"We all know that chocolate's bad for grown ups," Dennis chortled. "So I thought we should help the Colonel out!"

There was a flurry of hands and elbows, and a few minutes later the three menaces were surrounded by nothing more than piles of screwed-up gold paper. Pie Face gave a loud burp. "MMM! Chocolate – almost as delicious as pies!" he enthused.

"You know, Amazing Man's OK," said Curly, curling his hands over his chocolate-filled stomach.

"Yeah, and Mighty Man's all right," added Pie Face. "But we all know who the best, most menacing superhero really is!"

THE DAD FILES

Dennis was silent.

Curly and Pie Face were silent.

Even Gnasher was silent.

It was Pie Face's birthday, and he had just opened the most amazing present he had ever seen.

"Awesome," gasped Curly at last.

A slow grin was just starting to spread over Dennis's face.

"A secret agent kit!" he chuckled. "You know what this means? We've been given a licence to menace!"

There was a flurry of arms, legs and heavy boots as they all dived for the kit. Inside was a treasure trove of secret-agent gadgets – binoculars, skeleton keys, rope ladders, bugging devices, a miniature camera, not to mention a water-squirting watch and three walkie talkies.

Soon the gadgets were divided between the three menaces.

"Who's it from?" asked Dennis.

"My cousin," Pie Face explained. "He told me to open it away from Mum."

Dennis took a small black pad and a stubby pencil from his back pocket, licked the pencil and wrote MISSION 1 at the top of the page. Then he stopped.

"So what's the first mission?" asked Curly.

Dennis chucked two of the walkie talkies at Curly and Pie Face, then turned the third on.

"Stay in contact," he told them. "As soon as we get our first mission I'll let you know. Right now I've got a bit of work to do on my skateboard."

Dennis jumped onto his board and zoomed down the street, grinding along the kerb and making Mrs Perkins drop her shopping.

"Come back here, you menace!"

she yelled, shaking her fist so hard that her wig slipped to one side. But Dennis just whizzed around the corner and jumped over the gate into his back garden. He went straight into the shed and closed the door.

For the next hour there were some very peculiar sounds and smells coming out of that shed.

There were bangs and burps.

There were puffs of smoke and gloopy gurgles.

At last the shed door opened and Dennis came out with Gnasher at his side.

Dennis had his skateboard under one arm, a blob of oil on his nose and a very familiar gleam in his eyes. The shed was still gently smoking as he marched up to the house and let himself in at the back door.

Dennis peered through the kitchen door and saw Dad standing in the hallway, talking to someone on the phone.

"I have to keep my voice down," Dad was saying. "I just want to confirm the time. Seven o'clock – and make sure everything's ready!"

Dennis's eyes narrowed as Dad put the phone down. Gnasher frowned and looked up at Dennis.

"So, Dad's plotting something, is he?" mused Dennis. "No one's gonna keep a secret from me and my spies! Come on, Gnasher, we're on the case!"

Dennis raced out into the garden and pressed the button on his walkie talkie.

"Come in, agents! Can you hear me?"

"Loud and clear, Chief!" crackled Curly's voice.

"We've got our first mission!"

Dennis, Curly and Pie Face met in one of their dens in Beanotown Park.

Dennis told them all about Dad's mysterious phone call.

"He's up to something," Dennis finished. "And we're gonna find out what it is!"

"Brilliant!" said Pie Face.

"From now on, where Dad goes, we go," Dennis went on. "We've gotta stay out of sight and shadow him!"

"What are we waiting for?" bellowed Curly. "Let's go!"

They raced back to Dennis's house, just in time to see Dad walking down the garden path and carrying a large bag. Dennis stopped so suddenly that Curly and Pie Face bumped into him with a loud

192

SCRUNCH!

"OW! By doze!" groaned Pie Face.

"Shh!" hissed Dennis as Dad turned around. They ducked behind a hedge until he started walking again.

Walter's mumsy was tripping along the pavement towards Dad. Dennis grinned, waiting for Dad to cross the road to avoid her as usual. But then Dennis's mouth dropped open. Dad was hurrying up to her! He was stopping to talk to her!

"What's wrong with him?" gasped Dennis. "He can't stand Walter's mumsy! He always pretends to be asleep when she comes to gossip with Mum!"

Walter's mumsy was giggling. Then she nodded her head and made the pink fluffy flower on her hat wobble.

"Maybe he's asking for tips on how to turn you into a softy," Pie Face suggested. Dennis punched him in the arm.

"Maybe he's asking her if she'd like to adopt you!" grinned Curly.

"Har har," said Dennis with a smirk. "Maybe he's asking her to send Walter over to play at your houses!"

That wiped the grins off their faces.

Dad said goodbye to Walter's mumsy and carried on walking towards the shops.

"Have you got the binoculars?" asked Dennis. Pie Face pulled the binoculars out of his pocket and handed them to Dennis, who clapped them to his eyes. He was just in time to see Dad disappearing into the dry cleaners. Dennis, Curly and Pie Face scooted into the dairy opposite and peered out of the window.

"Very weird," muttered Dennis. Dad never ever went into the dry cleaners. In fact, Mum had said just the other day that she was still waiting for Dad to clean the suit he got married in.

Dennis looked through the binoculars, but all he could see was the bald patch on Dad's head.

He took a couple of pictures with his tiny secret-agent camera.

"What's he doing now?" asked Curly, trying to look through the binoculars. Dennis elbowed him out of the way and Curly trod on the dairy owner's in-growing toenail.

"YOWEEEEEEE! What are you troublemakers up to?" he bellowed. "Go on, get out. I know your dads!"

"Lucky him!" grinned Pie Face as they darted out of the door. "Look – your dad's on the move again!"

Dad had left the dry cleaners and was strolling down to the end of the street, whistling.

"He never whistles!" Dennis frowned. "There's something very fishy going on here. "Why is he so cheerful?"

"Maybe he's sending you to boarding school," said Curly.

"Yeah, right!" Dennis guffawed. "Like there's any boarding school in the country that would hold me!"

"Maybe he's going away to boarding school, and he took his old school uniform to the dry cleaners?" said Pie Face.

"Nah," Dennis replied. "He's way too ancient. Besides, you can't teach an old dog new tricks."

"GNASH!" agreed Gnasher.

"Hold it!" Dennis exclaimed, stopping suddenly. "He's gone into... I don't believe it!" He rubbed his eyes and shook the binoculars. "He's gone into the flower shop!"

"Urrgh," cried Pie Face.

"Yuck!" Curly grimaced.

"This calls for serious secret-agent action," said Dennis. He looked up at the roof of the flower shop. There was a window cleaner's ladder

leaning against the shop next door.

"Come on!" cried Dennis. He grabbed the ladder and raced over to the flower shop.

"OY!"
roared the
window
cleaner, who
had been up the
ladder. He was
now clinging to
the gutter with
his fingers.
"You bring that
ladder back
here now!
Help!"

"I'm Just
borrowing it!"
Dennis replied
as he leaned the
ladder against

the flower shop wall. "Come on, we've gotta hear what Dad's saying!"

Dennis, Curly and Pie Face dashed up the ladder and onto the roof, while Gnasher stayed on the ground to keep a lookout.

"Bark if there's danger!" Dennis told Gnasher. "Pie Face, where's that rope?"

Dennis tied one end of the rope around his waist and handed the other end to Curly and Pie Face.

Then he opened
the skylight and
peered down into
the shop. He could
see the top of Dad's
head and the
flower-shop
owner's curly red
perm, but he
couldn't hear what

they
were
saying.

"Lower me down
slowly!" Dennis
whispered.

Pie Face and Curly
took the strain and started to lower
Dennis down on the rope.

Dennis spread his arms and legs
out wide to get his balance, and
strained his ears to hear what Dad

200

was saying. He waved at Curly to lower him further.

On the roof, Curly and Pie Face were pink in the face. Beads of sweat were popping out all over their foreheads.

"A bit more!" puffed Curly. "Just a bit further!"

Inside, Dennis was getting closer and closer to the top of Dad's head. He snapped a couple more pictures of the bald spot. Dad nodded.

"That's all arranged then," he said. "But keep it quiet!"

Just then a pie van rumbled along the street past the flower shop. A wonderful aroma of hot pies wafted up to the roof and hovered under Pie Face's nose.

201

Pie Face's nose twitched.

It quivered.

Then it turned to follow the smell – and the rest of Pie Face turned too!

"Pie Face, I can't hold the rope myself!" bellowed Curly as the rope slithered through his hands.

CRASH! Dennis dropped like a stone, but luckily his fall was broken by the flower arranging table.

WHOOSH! Flowers of every size, shape and colour were catapulted into the air.

SNAP! The table cracked down the middle.

TING! The door tinkled as Dad left, unaware of what was happening behind him.

Dennis jumped to his feet and faced the flower shop owner. She had her hands on her hips and a plant pot upside down on her head.

"What do you think—"

Dennis darted out of the door and looked up and down the street, but Dad had vanished. Curly scrambled down the ladder and passed Dennis his skateboard.

Pie Face was disappearing into the distance behind the pie van.

"Did you see where Dad went?" Dennis said. "We've gotta follow him!"

"Oho, no you don't, you young rascal!" trumpeted a loud voice. Dennis and Curly turned to see the navy blue chest of Sergeant Slipper. "You're coming to the station with me to explain this flower fiasco!"

By now flowers were whirling all around the street and plant pots were rolling in the gutters.

"SCARPER!" yelled Curly and Dennis. Curly sped off in one direction while Dennis leapt onto his skateboard and made off up the high street.

"You don't get away that easily!" roared Sergeant Slipper. He jumped on his bicycle and gave chase.

Dennis just grinned and kicked a button on his skateboard. A jet of oil squirted out from the back of his board. Sergeant Slipper wobbled all over the road as his bicycle wheels skidded on the slick. With a loud yell he fell bottom-first into a puddle of oil.

"I'll get you, you menace!" Sergeant Slipper shouted, shaking his fist.

"You've gotta catch me first!" chortled Dennis. He kicked another button on his board and there was a roar of flames as his jet-propelled engine fired up.

"Every secret agent needs a getaway vehicle!" he chuckled to Gnasher as they sped away.

But as Dennis screeched around a corner he hit his neighbour the Colonel's toy soldiers, who were out on parade. The soldiers shot into the air like tiny rockets and **WALLOP!** One of them hit the Colonel in the eye.

"Insubordination! Revolution!" The Colonel hollered, grabbing the soldier as his eye started to swell. "It's the firing squad for you, my lad!"

"Quick, Colonel, have you seen my dad?" Dennis asked. But the

Colonel grasped Dennis's collar and his eyes popped out of their sockets.

"Your dad? Oh yes, I'll be seeing your dad all right! He'll be paying for a brand new regiment!"

Dennis struggled but the Colonel had him in an iron grip. Then he remembered the secret agent watch. It had been made to squirt water, but Dennis had made a few modifications to that, too...

"**AAARGH!** the Colonel shouted as he got an eyeful of cold custard.

"We're under attack! RETREAT! RETREAT!"

He let go of Dennis's collar and Dennis zoomed off at top speed, crunching more soldiers under his wheels as he went.

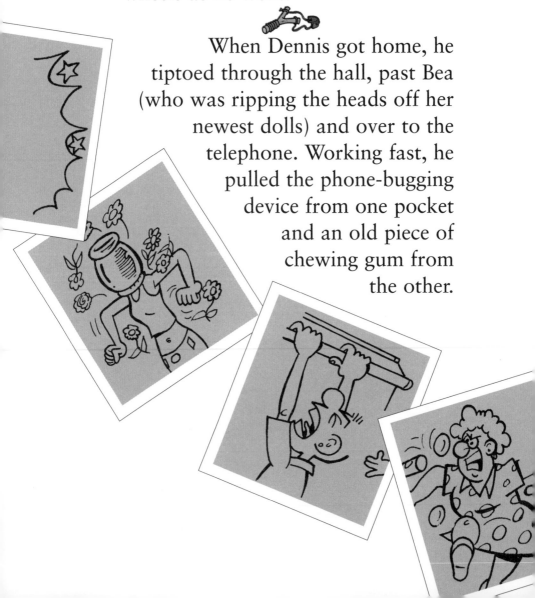

When Dennis got home, he tiptoed through the hall, past Bea (who was ripping the heads off her newest dolls) and over to the telephone. Working fast, he pulled the phone-bugging device from one pocket and an old piece of chewing gum from the other.

He quickly stuck the bug to the phone with the chewing gum. Then he went through the photos he had taken that day. Walter's mumsy, the dry cleaners, the flower shop... it was all very suspicious. And Dennis still had no idea what Dad was up to.

Dennis raced out to the garden and took up position behind the shed. Now all he had to do was wait for the phone to ring.

209

BEEP! BRRR!

Dennis clamped the listening device to his ear. But it wasn't Dad who answered the phone. It was Mum!

"Hello?" she said. Then she screamed. "YUCK! What's this on the phone? UGH! It's chewing gum! It's gone into my ear! DENNIS!"

Dennis darted out from behind the shed, but for once Dad had moved like lightning! He grabbed Dennis by the scruff of his neck and dragged him into the house. Mum was standing in the middle of the kitchen with the phone receiver chewing gummed to her ear.

"Get this off me!" she bellowed.

"Dennis, go to your room," said Dad. "And..."

(Dennis thought he knew what was coming.)

"... and change into your best clothes," finished Dad.

"Why?" Dennis demanded in amazement.

"Never you mind!" said Dad. "Just do it!"

Dennis stomped upstairs and slammed his bedroom door shut. If he had to wear his best clothes, that meant just one thing. A party. And judging by Dad's eccentric behaviour, he was gonna be inviting Walter's mumsy, which meant...

"Walter the softy's gonna be there!" choked Dennis in horror.

He pulled open his backpack and grabbed the rope ladder.

"No way am I getting into some stupid clothes and going to a party with Walter the softy," Dennis told Gnasher. He attached the ladder to the window ledge and unrolled it. "Sorry Gnasher, you can't climb down this ladder. I'll come and rescue you later when they've gone to the party."

"GNASH!" nodded Gnasher. Dennis sped down the rope ladder and darted off to find Curly and Pie Face.

It took Dennis a long time to find his secret agents. He tried the skate park, but they weren't there. He tried the high street and had to duck down an alleyway to escape Sergeant Slipper. He tried the toyshop, but only the Colonel was in there. (Dennis created a distraction by toppling a display of crying dolls over.) He even tried the pie shop, but there was no sign of them. Finally he remembered the walkie talkies, pushed the button and spoke into it.

"Curly! Pie Face! Can you hear me?"

"Loud and clear!" crackled Pie Face's voice. "Er, Dennis—"

"We've got a rescue mission!" Dennis interrupted. "Gnasher's stuck in my bedroom at home and we've gotta get him out!"

"**DENNIS!**" bellowed Curly and Pie Face together.

"OY!" roared Dennis, rubbing his ear.

"Gnasher's not at your house!" said Pie Face. "You'd better come and meet us. We're outside the Hairless Cat. Hurry!"

Dennis jumped on his skateboard. The Hairless Cat was the most expensive restaurant in town. It had just been opened by Gregory Ripples, the celebrity chef, and it was so exclusive that hardly anyone could afford to go there. What were Curly and Pie Face doing there?

Dennis screeched to a halt when he saw his friends outside the twinkling lights of the Hairless Cat. They were alone.

"So – where's Gnasher?" he asked.

Pie Face and Curly just pointed. As Dennis followed their fingers his mouth fell open. Sitting around a table in the window of the Hairless Cat were Mum, Dad, Bea... and Gnasher!

"I chased that pie van all over Beanotown," Pie Face explained. "Its last delivery was here – and that's when I saw them!"

"We managed to put a bugging device on Bea's dummy," added Curly, handing the listening device to Dennis.

Dennis put the listener in his ear and over the sound of Bea sucking her dummy, he heard Dad say, "Happy anniversary, Mum!"

"I can't believe you arranged all this!" Mum simpered. "Such beautiful flowers – and you got your suit cleaned!"

"I asked Walter's mumsy for advice about a present," added Dad.

"I love my new earrings!" Mum giggled.

"Oh no," Dennis groaned. "It was all for their anniversary. I've wasted all that menacing time and missed a slap-up feed!"

"I dunno about missing out on menacing," said Pie Face. "There was the window cleaner, the flower shop..."

"...Sergeant Slipper..." added Curly.

"... and the Colonel," agreed Dennis. "I guess secret agents are really just menaces in disguise!"

Suddenly there was a loud bark and Dennis looked down. Gnasher was standing at his feet, and in his jaws was...

"A Hairless-Cat doggy bag – from my hairy doggy!" yelled Dennis.

"Awesome!" grinned Pie Face

And the three secret agents tucked in to their own slap-up meal!

THE HOUND OF THE MENACES

It had been a long, soggy and annoying day.

That morning, Dad had decided that what the whole family needed was a long walk in the countryside. He had ignored Bea's wails, grabbed Dennis before he could do a runner and driven them all out to the Beanotown moors. It was too far to walk back and Dad had locked the car, so Dennis had no choice. He pulled on his wellies, hunched up his shoulders and stomped off after Mum, Dad and Bea.

First it had rained.

Then it had hailed.

Then it had rained and hailed at the same time.

"I am NOT HAPPY!" Dennis had growled, trudging along behind Mum and Dad.

"GNESH," agreed Gnasher.

"This will build character!" said Dad.

"I've GOT character," grumbled Dennis.

"Come on!" said Mum cheerfully, as rain streamed down the back of her neck. "Just two more miles and we'll stop for a nice spam sandwich!"

"What's wrong with a dry house, a bag of sweets and a comic?" Dennis groaned.

"Fresh air is good for you!" bellowed Dad.

"It might be good for parents," said Dennis, "but it's definitely not good for menaces!"

When they had finally got back to the car, it was starting to get dark and they were all soaking wet. Dad refused to look at the map because he said he knew the way home. After about ten minutes they were completely lost.

"We should have turned left at that signpost!" fumed Mum.

"We did!" Dad exclaimed.

"Well we should have turned right, then!" argued Mum.

On the back seat, Dennis was giving Bea a few quick menacing lessons and sharing a bag of glow-in-the-dark sweets with Gnasher. He fired a lemon drop at Bea with his peashooter and she dodged it expertly.

"You're getting pretty good!" said Dennis, impressed, as the lemon drop shot into Dad's left ear. The Menace grinned and Bea giggled as his luminous teeth shone.

"These glow-in-the-dark sweets are awesome," Dennis chuckled.

"Perhaps we should stop and ask for directions?" suggested Mum as she pulled the lemon drop out of Dad's ear with a loud POP! "We just passed an old hostel – they should be able to help."

Suddenly there was a worrying sort of KERDUNK from the car's engine. The car began to shudder and slow down. Then the engine stalled completely and the car rolled to a standstill.

Dad's knuckles went white as he gripped the steering wheel.

"Broke down! Broke down!" Bea sang, whacking the back of Dad's head with her rattle.

"There's a phone box just up there," said Dad. "I'll go and call the repair services."

Dad clambered out of the car and Mum watched him make the call. She saw him go purple in the face. She saw him waving his arms around and shaking his fist at the receiver. Then he slammed it down and strode back to the car. His left eye was twitching, which was a bad sign. He got back into the car and glared at Dennis.

"The emergency services aren't coming," he said. "They've got a very big file on this family. The man I spoke to asked if Dennis was with us. When I said he was, do you know what he said?"

"What?" asked Mum.

"NOTHING!" bawled Dad. **"HE HUNG UP!"**

"Excellent menacing result!" chortled Dennis.

"So, to sum up," said Mum, who had been looking forward to a nice cup of tea when she got home. "We've broken down on a stormy night in the middle of the moor and no one is coming to rescue us."

"We'll just have to push the car home," said Dad.

"Oho no!" said Mum. For a

moment she looked just like Dennis. Dad's knees trembled. "We are going back to that hostel and getting beds for the night. In the morning you can call a local garage to fix the car. But I am not pushing the car all the way back to Beanotown, and that's final!"

Ten minutes later they were dripping rainwater all over the entrance hall of the crumbling old hostel. There was no one in sight, but there was a large bell on the reception desk. Dennis picked it up and rang it.

CLANG!

Immediately a door opened behind the reception desk and a man peered out at them. He had a long, curving nose and jet-black hair slicked back with greasy gel.

"It's Count Dracula!" chortled Dennis to Gnasher.

"I'm Mr Mulch, the owner," said the man. "What do you want?"

Mum explained what had happened.

"All the rooms are taken," snapped Mr Mulch. "You can't stay here."

"There must be somewhere we could sleep!" Mum exclaimed. At that moment the door opened again and a woman stepped out. She had narrow eyes and long black ringlets that coiled around her face like snakes.

"This is my wife," said Mr Mulch. "My dear, these people want a room for the night."

"The only space is out in the garden," said Mrs Mulch hoarsely. "There are a couple of tents out there. But it will be a cold, stormy night. It would be better if you found somewhere else."

"Oh, er, well perhaps we should go…" stammered Mum.

"No way, this place is cool!" Dennis exclaimed, looking around at the cobwebby old building. "I wonder if it's haunted!"

"The garden will be fine," said Dad, glaring at Dennis.

"You've missed dinner," said Mr Mulch. "We can't feed you."

"That's all right," said Mum. "I've got plenty of spam sandwiches left over."

Bea curled her lip.

"I'm not sure we should let you stay out in the garden," said Mr Mulch. "It's on just such a night as this that the Hound of the Moor walks!"

"Pardon?" gulped Dad.

"The Hound of the Moor!" hissed Mrs Mulch. "A terrible red beast that stalks the moor on stormy nights, searching for prey!"

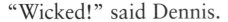

"Wicked!" said Dennis.

"Oo-er," said Mum.

"Its howls make your blood run cold," Mrs Mulch continued. "And its luminous jaws shine in the moonlight."

"They say that if you see its jaws, it will carry you off and you will never be seen again!" added Mr Mulch.

There was a long silence.

"I'd like to meet it," said Dennis.

"Me too!" smiled Bea. "Nice doggy!"

"The tents will be fine," said Mum. "We'll take them."

Mr Mulch looked as if he wanted to argue, but he just took the money and handed them a torch.

"I'll show you the way," he snapped. "Follow me."

He led them through long, echoing corridors, with polished wooden floors and expensive-looking rugs.

"These would make awesome slides!" grinned Dennis. He backed up, ran towards the rug and then skidded down the corridor. **"GANGWAY!"** yelled Dennis, but Mr Mulch was too slow. Dennis crashed into him and they somersaulted into a table. The vase that was on the table shot into the air, smashed against the ceiling and showered everyone in tiny pieces of porcelain.

230

"You little menace!" shouted Mr Mulch, shaking the pieces of vase out of his greasy hair.

"Er, let's get out to the tents," said Dad, before Mr Mulch could say anything about chequebooks.

The hostel owner led them to the back door and turned a large key. The door swung open with a loud CREEAKK. Dad switched on the torch and they saw two tents in the garden.

"There are sleeping bags inside," said Mr Mulch. "Remember, if you hear the hound howling, don't step out of the tents! And whatever you do, don't go over to that part of the garden."

He pointed over to where a stone wall separated a small area of the garden.

"Wh... why not?" asked Dad.

"Because that's where we have found the hound's paw prints!" hissed Mr Mulch.

"Brilliant!" said Dennis. Mr Mulch glared at him.

"That part of the garden is out of

bounds!" he said. "No menaces allowed!"

He pushed them out into the garden and slammed the door shut behind them. They heard the big key scrape as he turned it in the lock.

"Right, come on Gnasher!" said Dennis, heading for the stone wall. But a hand gripped the back of his neck.

"Oh no you don't," said Dad. "You heard what Mr Mulch said. You're not allowed over there, so get into your tent and go to sleep!"

"No way!" said Dennis. "Mr Mulch is hiding something and I wanna know what it is!"

"Buried treasure!" Bea gurgled.

"Rubbish!" Dad replied. "It's very kind of them to let us stay when they have no rooms free!"

"It is funny though," said Mum.

"This place is very well furnished for a hostel. Did you notice those expensive rugs? And that vase must have cost a fortune!"

"Shhh!" said Dad, thinking of his chequebook again. "Let's just go to sleep!"

Mum and Dad took Bea into one tent with them, while Dennis and Gnasher shared the other. There were no lights on in the hostel and the only sound came from the canvas of the tent shaking in the wind. Soon Dad's snores were rumbling around the garden. Dennis sat up and grinned at Gnasher.

"Come on!" he said. "I bet Bea's right! The Mulches have probably got stacks of treasure buried in this garden. Let's go hunting!"

They crept out of the tent and Dennis headed for the stone wall, but suddenly Gnasher stopped and began to dig in the red clay in one of the flowerbeds.

"What have you found?" asked Dennis in excitement. He helped Gnasher dig until at last they found...

"An old bone!" exclaimed Dennis. "HUMPH! We're looking for treasure, Gnasher!"

Dennis and Gnasher wandered all over the garden, digging holes in the flowerbeds and searching for treasure. They found a few more bones, a broken watch, fifteen pennies and a hedgehog having a late-night stroll, but no treasure.

As they were starting another hole, it started to rain. Soon they were happily plastered in thick, red mud. Then they heard a noise. It sounded like a key turning in a lock.

"Someone's coming out of the back door!" whispered Dennis. "Hide!"

They dived behind a bush and saw a torch bobbing across the garden towards them. As it passed them, they saw that it was carried by Mr Mulch! Mrs Mulch was close behind him, wearing a long black dressing gown that flapped in the wind.

"Come on,"
whispered Dennis. He and Gnasher
followed the Mulches across the
garden and past the stone wall.
When Dennis peered around the
corner, he saw a very strange sight
indeed. Behind the wall was a huge
cage, and it was full of bats!

"Weird-looking bats!"
said Dennis.
They weren't black like normal
bats. They were covered in white
splodges!
"You are a genius!" Mr Mulch
was saying to his wife. "What a
wonderful idea! To cross bats with
magpies!"

Mrs Mulch rubbed her hands together. "With the magpie's love for shiny things, our magbats will be able to steal things in the dark!" she cackled. "We'll be rich. RICH!"

"Bonkers," Dennis whispered, shaking his head.

"When will they be ready to steal for us?" asked Mr Mulch.

"We have to train them first," said Mrs Mulch. "And the best time for training magbats is at night!"

Gnasher was furious. He couldn't keep quiet any longer.

"GRRROWWWLL!" he rumbled, stepping out from behind the wall. The Mulches whirled around. Gnasher bared his teeth and stuck all his fur on end. Mr Mulch went white and Mrs Mulch screamed.

"It's the Hound of the Moor!" they shouted together. Gnasher's teeth were still luminous from the glow-in-the-dark sweets and his fur was red with mud!

Mr and Mrs Mulch dropped the torch and ran for the hostel, but in the dark they didn't see that Gnasher and Dennis had been digging.

"AARRGGHH!" yelled Mr Mulch as he stumbled into a flowerbed.

"EEEK!" squealed Mrs Mulch as she landed headfirst in a hole.

"Har har," sniggered Dennis, as he opened the cage. "Serves 'em right!"

The magbats swarmed out of the cage and flapped gratefully around Gnasher and Dennis, squeaking loudly. Gnasher howled "Don't mention it!" as lights started to go on all over the hostel.

Curtains were flung open and faces appeared at all the windows. They saw a terrifying sight! Mr and Mrs Mulch were upside down in the flowerbeds and there was a muddy boy-shaped monster leaping around the garden. Worst of all, the red Hound of the Moor was standing right outside the hostel, howling and baring his terrible glowing fangs! He was surrounded by a swarm of black-and-white bats that looked ready to attack – and there was a family in the tents nearby!

Screams came from every window in the hostel. Men fainted and women hid under the beds. No one noticed Dad peering out of his tent. No one saw him grab Dennis and Gnasher. No one spotted Dennis and his family racing back up the road to their car.

Dad turned the key in the ignition and let out a sigh of relief as the car started up. Mum wiped beads of sweat from her forehead. Dennis and Gnasher stared out of the back window at the hostel. They could see the swarm of magbats flying away and a stream of people running out of the hotel in panic.

"The Hound has eaten an entire family!" screamed one woman.

"Then it vanished into thin air!" shouted a man.

Dennis chuckled and grinned at Gnasher.

"That was one of the best menaces of all time!" he chortled. "We found some treasure, freed the magbats and started a legend! But you know what was best of all?"

Gnasher shrugged and Dennis gave a big wink.

"We showed Dad that fresh air isn't so good for you after all!"

More Bumper BEANObooks fun...

1-84539-214-0

1-84539-213-2

1-84539-095-4

1-84539-096-2

... make sure you've got them all!

1-84539-097-0

1-84539-098-9

1-84539-204-3

1-84539-205-1

More Bumper meadowside 🍃 fun...

1-84539-202-7

1-84539-203-5

1-84539-215-9

1-84539-101-X

... make sure you've got them all!

1-84539-099-7

1-84539-256-6

1-84539-102-0

1-84539-100-4

YOU'LL MEET...

...EVERY WEEK IN

GNEEK! FOR THE BEST MENACING ON THE NET...

...CHECK OUT

www.beanotown.com

Written by RACHEL ELLIOT

Illustrated by BARRIE APPLEBY

published under licence by

185 Fleet Street, London, EC4A 2HS